present
tense

The publication of this book was supported with grants from the Oregon Arts Commission, Oregon Literary Arts and the John and Netta B. Parke Fund of the Oregon Community Foundation.

With grateful appreciation, CALYX acknowledges the following "Immortals" who provided substantial support for this book:

A & S Accounting
Helen Berg
Mina Carson & Mina McDaniel
Floyd & Beverly McFarland
Polly & Robert Rutledge

Cover art, "Theresa," by Lara Karn Frankena
Artist's Statement: *"I use images to narrate what I know, what I remember. I am interested in how repression and denial anesthetize language. When language becomes stagnant, objects and images remain and become pregnant with meaning. By using the objects that are integral to a story, I can present what there are no words for."*

Cover & book design by Cheryl McLean and Micki Reaman

CALYX Books are distributed to the trade through **Consortium Book Sales and Distribution, Inc., St. Paul, MN, 1-800-283-3572.** CALYX Books are also available through major library distributors, jobbers, and most small press distributors including: Airlift, Baker & Taylor, Banyan Tree, Bookpeople, Ingram, Pacific Pipeline, and Small Press Distribution. For personal orders or other information write: CALYX Books, PO Box B, Corvallis, OR 97339, (541) 753-9384, FAX (541) 753-0515; for book orders only call toll-free: 1-888-FEM-BOOK (1-888-336-2665).

The paper in this book meets the guidelines for permanence and durability of the Committee on Production Guidelines for Book Longevity of the Council on Library Resources and the minimum requirements of the American National Standard for the Permanence of Paper for Printed Library Materials Z38.48-1984.

Library of Congress Cataloging-in-Publication Data
Present tense : writing and art by young women / edited by Micki Reaman, Amy Agnello, Maria Francesca Braganza, Sonia Gomez, Laura McFarland, Zola Mumford, Teri Mae Rutledge, Mira Shimabukuro, and Megan Smith.
Includes bibliographical references; indexed
    ISBN 0-934971-54-4 (alk. paper). —ISBN -934971-53-6 (pbk.: alk. paper)
      1. American literature—Women authors. 2. Young women—United States—Literary collections. 3. Feminism—United States—Literary collections. 4. American literature—20th century. I. Reaman, Micki
PS508.W7P73 1996
810.8'09287—dc20

96-24820
CIP
p. cm.

Printed in the U.S.A.
9 8 7 6 5 4 3 2 1

present tense

writing and art by young women

edited by Micki Reaman, Amy Agnello, Maria Francesca Braganza, Sonia Gomez, Laura McFarland, Zola M. Mumford, Teri Mae Rutledge, Mira Chieko Shimabukuro, Megan Smith

CALYX BOOKS ■ Corvallis, Oregon

Contents

Editors' Foreword

MICKI REAMAN

When CALYX began twenty years ago as a voice for women, I was thirteen; some of the women of *Present Tense* weren't even born.

Now, we are creating our own zines, our own literary journals and organizations, our own small presses. We are writing and seeing our words in print. We are making art and making it visible, any way we can.

Some of us are joining the women who founded the feminist publishing and book movement. Ever since I came to CALYX five years ago, I've experienced the struggles facing the next generations of feminist and independent publishers, the challenges and rewards of working with an organization that's been around the block. These are natural places for dialogue; we understand that communication is essential. *Present Tense* arose from the energy of younger women at CALYX; we are finding ways to make the work we do relevant to our (many-gendered) sisters, to make the publications we help create represent our stories.

A loud presence connects all the poetry, art, and prose gathered in *Present Tense*. These artists and writers are engaged; they resist stereotype. They grapple with serious issues in a complex way, creating art as it is always created at its best: from deep within. There is acknowledgement of the past, of the impact of history and family and culture on lives. Not all the contributors might name themselves "feminist," but an emerging—an *emerged*—aware and conscious and engaged generation is exposed within these pages.

Younger women are moving into the academic world, into small presses and mainstream presses, into every place, making noise. Here they are, some of them, in *Present Tense.* Get used to hearing from them. Learn from them and get to know them; they're here to stay.

MIRA CHIEKO SHIMABUKURO

Generation X-er's, apathetic slackers, baggy/tight jeans, clunky heels, pierced navels, eyebrows, tongue and cheek. Daughters of the women's, civil rights, and liberation movements, all out there trying to make sense of what's come before us, what we'll bring, what will follow.

I hear the long scream

voice gnawing at me from the inside

nothing to say for myself

swallowing the language

For me personally, working on the project made a trying first year on my MFA much more survivable. Struggling through more of the Canon than I ever had to before, it was easy to fall into severe periods of self-doubt. Some of my favorite work used metaphors that were labeled "ridiculous," or were written by someone who "still had a lot to learn."

wind made visible

> *I write/to remember/ these fragments*

I'm all camouflaged

> *my father is suspicious of my wardrobe*

These are the moments anthologies like *Present Tense* are needed. They save our lives, saying what some part of us has needed to hear aloud for a long time. Clenched teeth, open arms, whispered breath, they remind us we're not alone, encourage our strength, challenge us to survive.

AMY AGNELLO

When I talked to acquaintances and friends about this project, many looked almost puzzled by the fact that we sought the work of young women. Is that necessary, is there anything unique to be found in a collection of writing and art by young women living in America?

Thanks to the media, the youth culture of today is a greater part of the mainstream than ever before, propagating monolithic images that don't exist in reality. The general public looks at these images, whether it's rap or Riot Grrrl, and condemns us for our believed indulgence, self-centeredness, apathy, and, worst, the perceived thanklessness we extend to preceding generations. These images do not represent pieces I've read over the past nine months. The work confirms that the world outside this celluloid vision is alive and well.

In *Present Tense* young women pay their dues just as all the women who came before them. The women in these pages are still at the mercy of the cultural rules, institutions, and epithets that the founding mothers of feminist publishing encountered. They are all on the front lines of life, fighting to maintain their place at the table. Indeed the richly varied life experience of these women is what makes the collection unique.

In my work outside of editing, as an advocate for domestic and sexual violence victims, I encounter women of every strata imaginable. While this movement of survivors and friends took hold, women's publishing was being forged in the same kitchens and college campuses. The younger generation has reaped the benefits of nearly thirty years of struggle. We have also inherited the struggle in an era of unprecedented scarcity of funding and violence. Undaunted, the writers, artists, and editors of *Present Tense* reaffirm that our presence is a force to be reckoned with and I am proud to be in such company.

ZOLA M. MUMFORD

Some, speaking of young and youngish people, suggest that apathy, nihilism, and cynicism are part of a fashionable face for our generation to wear. The energetic, witty, intelligent, and empathetic young women who co-edited and contributed (there was just too much girlfriend power there to suggest that anyone "submitted") work for consideration in this anthology showed the exciting flip side to this stereotype. During hundreds of hours of reading, viewing artwork, and discussing this project with the editorial team, I knew that I was in good company. I love good anecdotes, the Internet, writing, making media, dancing, and I sometimes become fascinated by other folks' conversations on the bus; I like communication. The CALYX editorial collective process is one of the most effective I've ever seen: hard work, humor, and careful decision-making.

I know that the word "diversity" is taking a solid beating from both conservative and occasionally "progressive" sides these days, but I must mention it. This editorial collective was interesting in its diversity of ethnic identity, class/economic background, educational experiences, sexual orientation, day job vs. life work, creativity, and the other, subtler factors which shape a person. All had a healthy sense of irony, which I find so much more intriguing than flat cynicism.

I always looked forward to the meetings, knowing an exciting and productive exchange of ideas would take place. I always felt a part of the group. I grew up as part of the Pacific Northwest's small but hardy African-American community. My parents, both of whom were raised among the rural Black working class of the racially segregated South, were in the habit of taking my brother and me along with them to demonstrations. Perceptive and thoughtful little leftist kids, we watched public television and we learned when to avoid crossing a picket line. My parents had come from country families where everyone worked; my father put tools *into* my hands; he never took them out. The blend of country common sense and civil-rights era commitment helped me grow up feminist. Mom, who is now a writer and historian, was barred from entering the public library as a teenager; she made sure her children were devoted to the library, and she and my father filled our house with books.

Reading offered me knowledge of history, accomplishments, and achievements, a world where little Black girls, *all* girls, could do anything. Working with CALYX is an extension of my commitment to feminism, and my appreciation of women's creativity. Readers of this anthology will be in good company, too.

MARIA FRANCESCA BRAGANZA

I have worked with a fabulous group of women on *Present Tense*, and it's been a pleasure. As an emerging artist, I have helped create/imagine this journal in my role as an art editor.

I believe the role of the artist is to liberate: our minds, our eyes, our spirit. You won't necessarily *be* liberated if you see good art; sometimes it's just the opposite. The artist is a visionary and a communicator; she shows us things that make us pause, think, feel, relate, remember, reflect, recoil. I think sometimes the work of young women artists reflects a quest, reflects our lives.... We are not "there" yet, we are trying to find "it" (something). And find it we do—my eyes and mind click ("aaahhh"); the artist expresses the search and the object of the search eloquently. She has arrived.

Just as there are as many types of feminism as there are individuals who consider themselves feminists, there are as many forms of art as there are artists. I like to take people on their own representations as they create themselves, their lives, their life's work. I am pleased by the diversity of subject, form, and message in the art (and writing!) of *Present Tense*.

MEGAN SMITH

Maria and I sat in small dark rooms for many hours clicking through slide after slide of artwork. It was a rare opportunity to be there. I felt honored, but also experienced a twinge of guilt, as if I were hidden in a closet with some stolen journals and a flashlight, nosing around other women's souls. After all, I believe the raw material for art comes from the emotional heart of a life.

So I would remind myself I had been invited to be there, and that this art was created by women who value their unique perspective and manner of expression enough to want it in the spotlight. These are women who demand *not* to be invisible. They demand to be heard and say that what they create is valuable. These women shape for themselves what it means to be a woman, and in doing so they provide a strong model for future female generations to do the same. With this in mind, I viewed each slide with great respect.

For me, successful artwork does two things. When a theme is present in a piece that reflects something from my own life, it touches on something familiar that strikes up a kind of inner resonance. But also there must be something unfamiliar, something that makes the expression uniquely the artist's. It gives a twist to what I know and thereby enriches my own experience. All this happens in a nonverbal domain, in a space where the cognitive, plodding consciousness is not in charge, and the emotional and irrational part of ourselves can take precedence.

We chose artwork that compels. It does something within. It moves us some-how. It lets us revel in a realm where we are free to feel in undefinable ways with-out having to explain why.

SONIA GOMEZ

When Amy first asked me to be in on the twentieth anniversary issue, I was de-lighted. I was intrigued by the prospect of reading the words of women my age, and I also knew that this meant an opportunity to work with CALYX-women, a marvelous breed of people who, I knew from experience, would work hard as horses and have hearts the size of houses. All through the fall we read packet af-ter packet of prose and poems, and then through the winter came the signal-red-second-cut packets. What impresses me about the works that we finally selected is their voices are committed and daring. As a young poet and teacher of poetry, I know that writing is about commitment to both your subject and to the craft, the form that will chisel out shape. It's the struggle with issues of craft and the sheer will to voice, I think, that gives these works their compelling energy. I read this as a collection bristling with trajectories of thought—evidence of a genera-tion of sharp-minded and sharp-tongued, difficult women. Working on this project gives me a sense of history. What defines us as a generation? The answer I read in the collection is that we defy categories any way you look at it. I'm ready to keep writing.

TERI MAE RUTLEDGE

CALYX recently won the Oregon Governor's Award for the Arts. We were hyper-excited to attend the awards ceremony. It's not every day we get to eat seventy-five-dollar dinners.

I mashed my feet into pumps, found a tube of lipstick, put on a dress. Wore a bra. After all, it was a special occasion.

Sometime after my second glass of free champagne, my fearless leader Margarita Donnelly, resplendent in multicolored rayon, began to thrust me upon *important* people.

"Teri Mae can tell you what it's like being an editor at CALYX—tell Mr. So-and-so about the young women's anthology," Margarita would chirp before skipping off to locate the *really important* people.

For my part, I tried to remember what their acronyms stood for. I licked my teeth. I did not conspicuously adjust my bra. I talked about my involvement with CALYX and about editing the anthology. I exuded charm, independence, filial spunk, worship of the work ethic.

I found that most of this effort was superfluous, as long as I mentioned my age.

Being an editor at twenty-four seemed to make me, in that setting, a sort of child prodigy. A female Doogie Howser. It caused serious dissonance that a member of Generation X was wearing pink and smiling. Being the good promo girl that I am, I milked that.

It's a good thing I didn't have Emily Regan Wills' (age fourteen) essay with me. It's a good thing I didn't happen to have Julianna Parr's portfolio on me.

I'm not sure that a public setting would be the best for the scale of revelation the "arts world" will have when they see the work of *Present Tense*. I'm glad that me, my salmon-colored garb, and lipstick-less teeth were able to prepare them, at least a little bit, for the shock that's to come in these pages.

LAURA McFARLAND

I'm the only editor in this collective whose mother works for CALYX. Eight years ago she answered an ad soliciting volunteers in the local newspaper. My first reaction when she mentioned the ad was, "Something is published in Corvallis?" It still surprises me to read a submission by someone in England or Israel or Australia, or come across the journal in a bookstore in Texas, or get a letter from a reader in New York. I think, "I get to do this? They're writing to me? In *Corvallis?*"

For the first three of those eight years, I was away in college; I'd drop by the office on vacation or read whatever manuscripts my mother was reading at home, out of boredom as much as curiosity. My mother spent an inordinate amount of time reading, copyediting, and proofing manuscripts at home; CALYX manuscripts stacked everywhere were just a simple fact of life. Ultimately the oddest thing about working with my mother was that I started to call her by her first name because it just doesn't do to address someone by "Mom" in editorial notes.

After college, I lived in Corvallis for a year and became the youngest—by about fifteen years—member of the editorial collective. I was relieved when Micki told me that CALYX had decided to put together this current issue.

Some of the *Present Tense* collective's discussions have centered around the idea of, "How are we defining ourselves *compared to them?* Does the writer, the poet, the artist, really believe this, or did they come to their belief/idea/form as just a reaction?" But I think, really, it does a disservice to all that we are publishing to not get beyond those terms. The writer builds the poem, helps make it what it is—but you have to take motivation, inspiration, background into consideration always. It has to all go together: the history, the meaning, the sound, the way the words feel, the curve of a sculpture, the light in a photograph. A work of art is not composed of little parts that stand alone; a work of art is a composition of time and space and light.

Excisions of the Flesh

"Lucky come Hawaii."
Lucky come Hawaii, you say, Great-Grandmother.
But it wasn't luck that brought you here.
It was your body
they needed.
Hoe hana, Kalai, Hole Hole, Hanawai.
Kachi den. Hapai ko.
They needed your body.
You were the one who cultivated and weeded.
You irrigated and stripped and carried and loaded the cane.
I was there, Great-Grandmother—and I remember.
I remember the silt
from the dry red earth
around your mouth,
buried in the leather cracks
of your forehead.
I remember your sweat,
how it pulled your denim coveralls
and checkered blue cotton rag tighter
to your skin.
You squinted your eyes
tight until you could see again,
using your arm as a towel.
I remember the knuckles of your hands.
White around a wooden handle,
churning the earth.
Turning it over and over.
I remember the burns and stings of blisters
and cracked calluses as salt
seeped from your pores. Both your hands

lined with sweat and clay
you were unable to wipe away....
But Great-Grandmother, I remember.
I remember because I was there.
My body remembers.

i. Ankle

You were clothed with only a beautiful head of black hair and an ID bracelet around one ankle. Once a year—on my birthday—my mother tells me about the first time she saw me. Her water breaks and it isn't until twenty-one hours and twenty-eight minutes of labor later, white sheets dark with sweat beneath her back, neck, and head, that I emerge from her body.

You're fine, mama, you're just fine, an orderly soothes, smoothing long trailing wisps of black hair away from her glistening face. *Where's my baby? Where's my baby?* Men in long white coats and identification cards drift in and out of the hollow room, inspecting her urine, taking blood pressure and hammering at her legs to test the reflexes of her knees. They fill her veins watery cool with clear bags of Pitocin and oxytocin. *Where's my baby? Where's my daughter?* She calls for me through the liquid numbness, certain I will be a girl.

Daughter.
My daughter.
Last night I had the dream again.
The dream from which I've awoken
into the darkness so many nights before, the yellow
moonlight through the curtains, filtered in waves
across my sleeping body
and the mountain of my womb.
I dream of us.
You and me, daughter,
and we are talking. Just talking.
And you aren't a teeny baby
but a miniature person
and we speak in a language
that no one else can hear or understand.
Our mouths

are moving. Our lips
shaping words that we toss
through the air only to each other.
And I knew from this dream—
like I've known all along—
that a baby who came out talking
had to be a daughter.

The red horizontal line of the fetal monitor blinks from across the white-walled room and my mother calls to the orderly to spread the curtains wide to let the twilight in. As the metal rings slide horizontally across the bar, her eyes search the horizon. Past the "Live Girls" in cursive neon pink. Across the four-lane highway and the pasture lined with wooden posts and barbed wire. And although her supine body remains amidst the starched and ammonia-streaked whiteness of the military hospital, she takes me with her to that point in the distance—that rising and dipping line of darkness where the sky meets the earth.

Today is my birthday and I sit facing my mother on the crushed yellow velvet of our living room sofa, ribbons and pink crumpled paper at her bare feet. My legs drape across the brown skin of her lap and she traces an imaginary circle around the base of my calf while she tells me—as she always does on my birthday—about the first time she saw me. *You were clothed with only a beautiful head of black hair and an ID bracelet around one ankle.*

ii. The Spot
The Mongolian Spot. From what my mother tells me, the Mongolian Spot looks like a big bruise on the small of your back when you're born. Not an indelible darkness, but more a shadow that looms suddenly and dissipates slowly, fading lighter and lighter until one day it is only a memory. Although I never knew at what point my mother's stories were inspired more by memory or imagination, I don't think she made this up. She and my grandma and aunties laugh about it, and whenever my mother runs into another Asian woman she always asks, *So, does your baby have The Spot,* which usually evokes laughter and stories and eye contact held a moment longer at the parting moment than if The Spot had never been mentioned.

The Spot, though, didn't show up until after I had been brought home and the white-haired neighbors—concerned—sent someone to the house. Men from the state knocked on her door with papers and fountain pens and clipboards and badges while she was out weeding the beauty bark around her roses.

> Questions. Polaroids. Measurements.
> I know what you're thinking.
> White-robed interrogator, I know why you're here.
> Write this on the black-lined paper you
> have clipped to your board
> and clutched to your chest.
> Tell them that I don't eat dog.
> That my feet aren't bound.
> That I speak English without an accent,
> that I don't roll my r's and l's.
> And make sure you write this word
> for word.
> That I would never hurt her.
> I would never hurt my
> daughter.

The Mongolian Spot. They took Polaroids of my back. My mother always described it as a long spiraling snake, and although I never saw the photographs I imagined a big black question mark. A beautiful curvaceous question mark winding around the small of my back. In sixth grade the science teacher gave us an assignment and I wanted to do my report on the Mongolian Spot, but as it turned out there just wasn't any information. I looked in the dictionary and the encyclopedia, but the only thing I could find had nothing to do with The Spot. I found out that Mongol could be an adjective meaning a native of Mongolia or of a contiguous region in East Siberia or a noun meaning a region in Central Asia. But what was really disturbing was that it's also a noun meaning a congenital disease characterized by mental deficiency, a broad face, slanting eyes, and a short fifth finger—the same as a Mongolian Idiot, a person having Mongolism. The preferred term, the encyclopedia reported, was now Down's Syndrome. *Down's Syndrome.* No way was I going to fuel my sixth-grade classmates with this kind of incriminating scientific evidence, so I abandoned these efforts. I did my report on the central nervous system.

The Mongolian Spot. A looming shadow question mark that dissipates slowly into memory. A bruise on the small of the back, from what my mother tells me.

iii. Eyes

When I was born I had blue eyes. I've heard all babies have blue eyes when they're born, but my eyes were deep silver blue, a permanent blue, a blue that my mother's heart could cave around, that could make her feel she had done something right, that she had submitted—finally—to my father's chromosomes. A blue that would let her forget about her own eyes, conspicuously and suspiciously brown and narrow and ultimately and irreconcilably foreign. Blue enough to make this land her land, blue and deep as the Pacific Ocean when it touches the white, sandy shore. Blue as the sky through white cotton candy clouds.

> *Blue Moon, aqua blue, blue velvet, you*
> *left me standing alone, baby blue, blue blood, bluebonnet,*
> *without a dream in my heart, blue chip,*
> *bluegrass, blueprint,*
> *blue sky, blue ribbon, without a love*
> *of my own, the lady sings the blues.*

One day when my mother had finished folding clothes and vacuuming and doing the dishes and taking the garbage to the end of the driveway, she walked to where I lay sleeping in my white bassinet under layers of pink and yellow crocheted afghans and stood over me, running the palm of her hand over the tufts of my black hair and the padded flesh of her index finger down my cheek, circling my tiny purse of a mouth and chin. She scooped me into her arms and tiptoed over to the window and when I blinked my eyes open she noticed, as the morning sun wilted through the lace curtains, that her reflection had turned from blue to brown. My beautiful baby-blue eyes were brown. Like hers. Brown like dirt. Brown like soil. Brown like the earth. The shifting, moving tectonic plates colliding and collapsing—earth.

Often I have thought that the Mongolian Spot was just a matter of biological fact. One day it was there and then it faded away without a trace of ever having existed. But my eyes. My eyes became my mother's first disappointment. Biology, I discovered as I grew older, was not so much a matter of fact as it was one of condition and circumstance.

> *Don't it make my brown eyes blue. Gonna*
> *make my brown eyes green. Stare into the sun.*
> *Don't blink.*
> *Don't cry. Bright white and blinding*
> *but don't turn away or close your eyes. An invisible*
> *hand lifting your chin*
> *to the sun, eyelids twitching with the brightness, the*
> *whiteness, the light*
> *is turning your brown eyes green. Close your eyes*
> *and the world is black*
> *and gray but your eyes are green. Slowly the colors*
> *will come back.*
> *They always do.*

In fourth grade I learned the word "chink." Even though I had never heard the word before, I knew what it meant. I remember. I remember we were all sitting around the orange circular table during lunchtime. I remember Eric was the first boy who ever made me blush just by being next to me. I always gave him my Snickers bar or tuna sandwich on white bread or whatever he wanted from my lunch. And even though my mother told me cheating was wrong, I always let him look at my paper during spelling tests. I always gave him my answers. But on this particular day he and the other kids were laughing and I tried to laugh along with them even though I didn't know what the joke was. The more I laughed, the more they laughed, until I didn't think it was funny anymore. And then they shook until Velveeta and bologna crumbs fell out of their gaping mouths. I placed my lunch back into my crumpled recycled brown paper bag and right before I got up I heard them say it. Well, Eric said it at least. I still remember how the corners of his mouth curved as he shaped the word into a ball, throwing it into the space between us where it exploded into a million pieces right there in the school cafeteria.

"Chink."

I tried to laugh again but my mouth was dry and I knew. Somehow I knew it wasn't really that funny. That day when my mother asked me how school went I said, Oh, it was fine, it was the same as always and by the way, Mom, what is chink? Her lips tightened over her teeth and she demanded coldly, as her knuckles whitened around the gear shift, why I wanted to know. Where did I hear that word? Oh, nowhere, Mom, I said. I was just wondering. Today we learned how to square dance at school.

Spin your partner 'round and 'round.

There were no boys left so I had to dance with Judy. The girl with dry hands like snakes.

Jack be nimble, Jack be quick.
Spin your partner 'round and 'round.

Next time, my mother said, the left turn signal blinking our car into the driveway, next time tell them it's Jap. Not chink.

Once my mother asked me what my earliest childhood memory was. I think I made something up, like I remember the way the yellow and orange linoleum glistened in the rusty glow of twilight and how my father would come home from work early in the summer in his brown Air Force uniform and I remember the metal pins reflecting the setting sun and I remember him taking off his hat and how he taught me to catch a ball in the backyard. I think I told her how I remember that the colors were brown and gold and how the long, burnt summer grass felt dry on my bare feet and swayed back and forth in the wind and how I remembered the chain-link fence that divided our backyard from the sprawling rolling field beyond.

I told her that, knowing it could easily have been my first memory, but it wasn't. It was a lie.

In my first memory I am sitting in the back of my father's lemon
yellow Datsun. Black, cracked vinyl interior sticking to the backs of
my legs, and I am prying my eyes wide with my thumbs on my
cheekbone and my forefingers pulling my eyelids towards the crown
of my head. I am stretching my skin tight across my face and it

hurts and my eyes are watering. The leather-covered metal buttons
of the seat are poking into my back as my father drives me to school
and I am pulling my eyes open.
Farther and farther.
I can change my eyes.

There's this funny thing I heard just the other day. Not ha-ha funny but funny in an ironic and disgusting way. During the Vietnam War, white American GIs thought that Asian women's vaginas were slanted. Like their eyes.

Hey there, baby.
Hey, yellow chicky baby.
Shake it. Shake it. Shake,
shake it, baby.
How much for ten dollars?
Hey baby, where're you goin'?
Don't turn your back to me.
You can run, baby, but you can't hide.
I'm comin' to get you. I know
you can hear me, baby.
Don't you turn your back on me.

So it all makes sense. Just last week I was sitting, drinking coffee. You know, minding my own business just drinking coffee, reading the classifieds, and this guy comes over and asks if the seat was taken. Nope, I said. What are you? he asked. Where are you from? And the silences at the end of each question that start as an impasse quickly become chasms. I can tell you're something—some sort of Asian—from your eyes. The rest of you could just be normal, but your eyes, yeah. They give you away. He proceeds to tell me that he's always wanted to date a Japanese woman. Their eyes are so...so exotic. He's intrigued, he says, by their eyes. That he just wants to get inside those eyes but they're so, well, *dark*. So, well, *impenetrable*. Do you know what I mean, he says, cocking his head slightly to the right, sipping his heavily creamed Americano. Yes, I say, folding the classifieds, tucking them under my arm and turning away to leave. To leave this place and leave him there. I think I do.

When I was born I had blue eyes. Eyes that are now conspicuously and suspiciously brown and narrow and irreconcilably foreign.

iv. Hands

My mother would shake her finger only inches from my face. *I don't like his eyes,* she would say when I brought boys home from school. *Just look at his eyes. How can you trust him?* She was always right—but Mother, I wanted to say, Mother, eyes don't always tell the truth. They can fool you sometimes.

But hands—hands never lie.

My hands look old for my age. These lines across my knuckles run deeper every day, it seems, and no matter how much lotion I use, my palms, which were smooth not so long ago, are now covered with calluses and white spiderwebs of dry skin. When I was young, I would squint at the twisting, rolling coils etched onto my fingertips. No fingerprint is the same, we learned in school. Not even identical twins'. And I imagined that the tips of my fingers were compasses guided not by magnetic force but DNA and chromosomes. And I wondered how closely mine would resemble my mother's when dipped in black ink and pressed onto a fresh piece of white paper. I wondered what would happen if I walked over to the stove while she was cooking and while her back was turned, what would happen—I only wondered—if I pushed my fingers down with all my weight onto the orange, glowing, coiling elements. Would I erase it all? How would they identify me with no fingerprint, nothing but a smooth and even smudge of black ink? And I wondered why the thought made me smile.

> *My hand cupped in yours, Mother,*
> *as you lead me down a winding path*
> *through the cemetery to the place where we will kneel upon*
> *the earth*
> *beside Great-Grandmother's grave.*
> *The knuckles of our hands*
> *touching beneath the cloudy, soapy water*
> *as I copy you, towing the rag*
> *through the water.*
> *Deeper, swirling.*
> *Swirling, surfacing.*
> *Wring the water out and scrub the granite headstone until the*
> *sun refracts*
> *and you see your reflection, shiny black.*

Eyes. Don't always tell the truth. They can fool you sometimes. But hands—hands never lie.

v. Heart

The entire twenty-one hours and twenty-eight minutes of my mother's labor our pulses were monitored by electrodes hooked to machines by long and winding wires. As her heart beat faster, so did mine. And the drugs flushed into her veins by needles and tubes swam through mine as well. *You're fine, mama. You're fine.*

Men in long white coats and identification cards drift in and out of the hollow room, inspecting and testing. Veins fill, watery cool. *Where's my baby? Where's my daughter?* She calls for me through the liquid numbness, certain I will be a girl.

Mother.
When I was young and you were sleeping
I would crawl like a cat
into your bed.
While you were sleeping, I would lie behind you
and trace the horizontal line of your sleeping figure
with my fingers, draping them along your body
as if they were raindrops falling
from the clouds and heaven onto the soil
of your dark silhouette.
With your comforter pulled up to your chin
in the morning darkness after Father left,
I imagined you were a sprawling mountain range
stretched across the horizon of your bed.
The rain falls over your feet, here. Your ankle, here.
Your calves, your thighs, your hip, here. Your belly, your elbow, here.
Your shoulder, here.
The rain cascades down your neck.
My fingers, water from the sky. Your body, earth.
Tell me your memories, Mother. I want to remember them, too.
I will remember.

Conceiving of Me

The story she tells stars herself,
as my mother-to-be, in a fuzzy pink
bikini, straddling a gigantic Coca-
Cola bottle. It wasn't her idea.
It was meant to be
something else: an outer
layer of Dante's *Inferno*. Heavy.
Deep. It's 1967. Interactive theatre.

Beneath her, an aspiring collegiate
Hercules surfs the tunnel between
her legs, mechanically in and out
and in again. His board's on tracks.
This is a sexual metaphor. Get it?
She didn't. Hard to believe.

My father-to-be is not the surfer;
he comes later. Literally.
This is unmistakable,
as explicit as it gets
on TV:

One thing leads to another.
Waves crash ashore like washed-
up metaphors; a train barrels
through a nine-month tunnel.

Meanwhile, she's an emotional
ocean, alone in Milwaukee,
full of sardines and the bulging
secret of me. She eats cheap,
lays low, catches what rolls in:
i.e. labor, the bus to the hospital,
her ride back afterwards.

Her water swells, crests, and
breaks: a wave.
Good-bye. Natural birth
can be described with a simile:
like Hell, it hurts.

I gush out headfirst and scream.
I am born without reason, small,
bald, and symmetrical. The usual:
ten fingers, ten toes,
nothing to say for myself.

Comiendoselo a los muertos (Eating Your Dead)

Guanajuato, México

You can't cut your eyes away
from the naked shrivel on velvet pillows,
mouths open like baby birds.
Tongues writing names in the space between lips,
the tracings half scrutable, wrapped,
the color of mummy.

Men in red, chewing loose threads in their jackets,
are calling through hands: forty years
hardened like molasses in the church cellar.

The absence of money swallows history,
and so, in glass caskets, the bloodless *Nieveblancas*
wrinkles yellow in a ring of dwarves:
a bouquet of farmers, pregnant women,
hitchhikers who never spoke the language.
Like your grandfather.

A B-movie appears each decade
starring enraged carnivorous piles of bandages.
Cuidado con las momias. Be careful.

Flashbulbs in a hallway,
the men flip their pancake narrations.
You breathe on the glass over a split mouth.
A resuscitation, or a feeding.

"*Cuidado,*" whispered in your ear.
A smirk curls on a red collar's edge.
Your skin takes on the texture of a jaundiced pastry
on the back shelf of the *panadería.*

You unravel on the far side of a doorjamb.
The mob of men waiting there wave good-bye
with taffy on sticks, yellow and limbed,
smiley-faced, fixed with straw hats.
Another calling through hands:
Llevense las momias a casa en el estomago.
Take them home with you in your stomach.
Like drinking crushed bones at an Aztec funeral.
The first part you eat is the head,
swallowing the language
of a dry and dreamless ancestor.

A Father's Child

for Fred Hampton, Black Panther murdered in his sleep

I heard about you the first time through my mother.
I heard of coal eyes set in milk chocolate skin;
I heard about the body chiseled out of struggle.
I heard your laughter in my mother's tears. No one knew
I heard the gun shot from where I was, placenta-wrapped
I heard, and fighting for my life already. She said,
"I heard you scream" as you struggled to survive. But
I heard the blood rushing towards the wall as bullets ricocheted.
I heard the bullet ring into your body and her scream: "Freddy!"
I heard about you through history. It doesn't matter that
I heard black man in black clothes means revolt, but poets,
I heard, wear black so their words stand out.
I heard sometimes they snap their fingers when they write revolution.
I heard that somewhere. I heard that somewhere.
I heard that your child has grown out of mourning the death of you.
I heard that police man is watching his shadow move into what
I heard would be your walk. He remembers you, police man, he remembers,
I heard, what your face looked like as you dreamed. Mother says,
"I heard your father's voice when you spoke. Did you hear? Did you hear?"

learning Philippine history

in first grade,
i learned
that some kano
said, "I'll be back."

but he never left
nor did the Spaniards
   cuz my history book
        is not mine
and baby Pepe Lito
will still be sold
tonight
by his parents
to a pimp
in Ermita.

in our bayan,
Pinoys join
the military
to master
the art of
corruption.

torture is
cheaply done
with
a cigarette,

a knife,
a fist,
a dick.

in our bayan,
our lolas in the north
will always
luhod in front
of their Spanish god,

clutching
their rosaries
praying
for
salvation,

but the Spanish god
is always taking siesta
in this
tropical heat.

in Mindanao,
the kano are not welcome
because
of DOLE,
the Smokey Mountain,
Pepe Lito,
and children
asking their
papa in Saudi

for stateside
tsokolate.

i write
to remember
these fragments
of realities
that i have
left

cuz CNN
tells me
that my
country is dead
and
People Power
is just another
revolution
in the Third World
that the Americans
help
win.

Aliens

Lola chews on ginger root
Remember, hija
chin up
back straight
and look them in the eye

> in Amerika
> everyone must know how to speak English
> even the dogs

me and kuya
seat belts buckled
fly to Amerika

> in Amerika
> everyone knows the name of the President's pet
> and who did you
> say killed Magellan?

remember
nickel is five
dime is ten
Is it penis or pennies?
I forget

> Where are you from again?
> Was it Taiwan? Japan? Thailand?
> I know it's one of Those. The what?
> Oh! The Phillipines? Don't WE have a Base there
> or something?

I pledge allegiance to the flag
of the United States of America
ta da ta da ta da for which
it stands one nation under
God indivisible ta da ta da ta da
and justice for all

Lola chews on guava leaves.

Notes:

bayan *is country or nation.*

DOLE *is the banana and pineapple plantation and company in South Cotabato, Philippines.*

Ermita, Olongapo City *was developed into a brothel city for the U.S. base.*

hija *is dear girl.*

kano *is an American.*

kuya *is older brother.*

lola *is grandmother.*

luhod *is kneel.*

Pinoys *are Filipinos.*

Saudi *is Saudi Arabia, where most of the Pinoy overseas workers are sent.*

Smokey Mountain *refers to one of the slum areas in Tondo, Manila, Philippines. Originally flat, mountains were formed from dumped garbage. The mountains are described as smokey because of the burning of the garbage.*

stateside *is what Pinoys call anything that is made in the U.S.*

tsokolate *is chocolate.*

NOSTALGIA   70" x 50"   **PRITI DAROOKA**
                                mixed media

My paintings deal with issues about a woman's role in Indian society, religious differences in India, inhuman exploitation, and abuse. I grew up in a sexist society. Girls are brought up to believe that their life's goals are to be good wives and good mothers and that they should be happy playing those roles.

A LANDSCAPE FOR MY MOM   70" x 50"   **PRITI DAROOKA**
                                   mixed media

Land is important to Indians. Being an agrarian country, land is the provider. Like a mother, she takes care of her children, and so is respected and referred to as the Motherland. The backgrounds of my paintings are often barren landscapes, the tortured motherland. Being female, the helpless motherland correlates to a woman's suffering. The barren landscape also expresses the irony of my nostalgia. I do miss home. I do long to go back. I am also aware of what my fate in India as a female would be.

Eastern Frontier

I had this image of life: a tall cabinet in my bedroom where I'd keep the flannel sheets and bath towels, with tiny compartments where I could store butterfly wings and broken glass. The room would have a rug so thick you'd want to sleep on the floor and pillows that let out a little gasp of air when you put your head down. And a stained-glass window—a purple center with four blue petals reaching for each corner in waves. While the sun hiked across the sky each day, warm rays would splash my floor in color.

I never saw Dub's stained-glass art until we moved together to Massachusetts, where it now sits above our kitchen sink, pouring green and brown onto the yellow counters. It was the first thing he'd hung when we moved to the trailer. Dub's grandmother had made it for him. He showed me it was a deer, pointing out the head and tail. The background was dark green with a couple triangles of light green that were supposed to be leaves. It looked more like the flowers I imagine his grandmother was used to making. But it struck me how Dub loved the thing, how he could see so much in what looked to me like a blob of brown in a mass of green.

I looked back at the stained glass in the lit window of the trailer as I twisted the lock on the door and stepped into the night. The sight of it reminded me how it felt when we first moved from Minnesota to Massachusetts, how we thought of ourselves as frontiersmen—probably because we were the only people we knew to move out of Webster's Crossing—though we were heading east instead of west.

When Dub was getting ready to head out to Towne Tavern tonight, I let him kiss me on the forehead, knowing full well that tonight was the night I would follow him there, to weigh his desire for us in his reaction to me. It took a minute for my eyes to adjust to the dim starlight, and I paused on the dirt driveway for a moment, watching my breath leave my body in frosty puffs. Before Dub left, he'd grabbed his camouflage jacket, slipped a bottle opener into his jeans pocket so he could open his own beer, and then turned to me.

"Just think," he said as he swiped his truck keys from the top of the fridge. "By this time next year you'll be able to come with me."

Dub used my age as a guise for going out unattended, though last year, before we lived together, before we moved, my age presented a challenge that he rose to. He outsmarted the bouncers at Margaret's, sneaking me in though the bathroom window until I became such a regular feature I was no longer hassled.

And I'll admit this: I wanted a reason to keep believing in Dub. I wanted to believe in the floor plans he sketched on placemats at the diner where we had Sunday breakfasts. I wanted to believe that someday I'd walk across smooth pine in moccasins he made for me from deer he hunted himself. When we had coffee each morning before work, we'd sit on lawn chairs in the chill air of our backyard, looking out over the expanse of land that surrounded our trailer, comparing it to what we'd someday own. Dub wanted me to have a garden with raspberries and asparagus, things that took years to grow.

My eyes adjusted to the night and I cut across the field-like grass of the side lawn to Red Holler Road and the mile stretch before it turned onto Miller Avenue, where I'd have three more miles to walk before I reached Towne Tavern. I could picture myself walking into the bar; I'd catch Dub's blue-green eyes and he'd say, Great to see you! Guys, look who's here! He'd pass me around to his friends, patting their backs as they shook my hand. He'd talk the bartender into serving me a beer, though I hadn't shown ID, then buy a round of drinks to toast me. I wouldn't stop him from spending our cable money on booze because life's life—it's once around.

As I started down the slope of Red Holler, I walked just off the shoulder, where the gravel gave way to spiny grass, and I thought about the two things in life I wish I'd never learned.

The first was about loons. I got fired from a job because I knew loons could stay underwater for a minute and instead of painting the trim on the cottage I kept counting. It bugs me; I want to know how long they can stay under without coming up. They're not like people, holding their breath, working against the grain to stay down as long as they can, finally breaking the surface, gasping for air. Loons go down for what they need and return to the surface, uncalculating.

The second was about my father, about why he left. I know it's not new that a man leaves for another woman, but my father seemed to leave for another life. At first, when he still lived in town, he'd take me and my sister Carrie to the fish fries on Friday nights, but it wasn't long before he moved out of state with a woman named Sarah Tillman. Part of me wishes that he'd left right away, so I wouldn't have known that his not looking back was a conscious choice.

As I started down Miller Avenue, the road widened and I could see a half-mile ahead where the streetlights started. There was one other thing I learned: not to bother Dub when he had it in his mind to go to Towne Tavern. I felt light-headed with the anxiety of possibility; I wanted Dub to react to me. I wanted to see pure emotion played across his face, instant, unexpected. I didn't want to wait for him every night; I didn't want to wonder if it was only a matter of time before he left. And I didn't want to pretend that what I was doing could be called living life.

There's a story I tell about my sister, about her and Larry—about their kid, their two bathrooms, and their four clotheslines. I tell it when anyone asks why I moved to Massachusetts, when anyone asks where I'm going in this life. I start off saying they had a beautiful ceremony, that I was the maid of honor and wore a long pink satin dress that gave me cleavage. I tell about how I helped stencil the kitchen of the 1890 farmhouse they moved into after their marriage, the house Larry saved enough money to buy.

Of course, I made the whole thing up, ignoring that Larry, like my mother, worked at the Cargill plant, that their wedding was an elaborate yet spontaneous trip to Nevada, that their trailer was not much different from the one I share with Dub. Still, I tell of their corn, or beets, and people just assume that since I'm from Minnesota, farmland pulses through my blood. I never talk about the 1.3 acres from which I was spawned, only of the peach trees on my sister's farm. I know the things grow in Georgia, but I tell of how the breeze catches the scent and drifts through the open windows to wake you just after sunrise (I have my own bedroom at the farmhouse), how Carrie and I go out on trails that stretch so far we walk for hours without seeing the end. There is so much fruit around us, we pull it from the tree and carry it home in sundresses we lift from the bottom to use as pockets. My sister, I tell in my story, is destined for six children and 780 acres, and has tallied thus far one and 230. So. I pause. It's a good life, if that's what you want.

■ ■ ■

While Dub was just as likely to turn his head to a skinny woman as the next guy, he truly appreciated my form. Said that he never met a girl before who could hold her own in a canoe. His dates before would go out on the lake with him, but they always wanted to go scrambling for shore at the first hint of waves. He could head down a river with me.

But that January day before we left Minnesota cemented it—barely a minute passed before the wind blew us clear to the middle of Cisco Bay and we were fighting to get back. Though I knew from the start we had no business going out there, I had this feeling about Dub, a feeling that while the earth kept spinning on its axis, Dub—with his tall, thin body pulled tight with muscle, his uncut hair, his red down vest pulled over his flannel shirt, turtleneck, and long johns—Dub would walk straight through this life, never finding himself on the wrong path, because he never stopped to wonder about it.

That day on the bay was the only time I'd seen Dub scared. It was just us and the canoe, fighting the wind and the chopping waves to turn around, then push hard to shore. We fought for a good ten minutes to turn, the whole time just barely maintaining the position we'd already earned. I told him that instead of working against the wind, we could ride it to the opposite side, then follow the shoreline back. And we did. By the time we got to the edge of pine, Dub was relaxed enough to see we were out of danger, relaxed enough to loop the rope around a tree trunk and crack open one of the beers we'd brought along. Sitting in the heatless sun of that January afternoon, safely anchored to a thick stub of pine, Dub told me he was ready to make plans.

When we first got to Clarke County, Dub would tell me his dreams one by one as we had our morning coffee, waiting for the sun. It seemed as if he had a lot of dreams then, a lot more than I'd ever thought about having. He thought if he just saved enough money, he could make stained glass. He knew how, he said; his grandmother had taught him. I remember thinking at the time that it didn't fit him, the man I knew from Margaret's, playing darts with Sampson and Dirk. Stained glass was art.

After he first told me this, I started collecting glass. Not that I knew what to do with the stuff. I just had a feeling that if I had enough of it, I could melt it down, make something beautiful. I usually stopped at the Food Lion parking lot on my way home from babysitting, put on my Isotoner gloves, and biked in slow circles until I found a patch of greens or browns, mostly around the outskirts of the lot—bottles broken by teenagers partying on the weekends. Picking up the pieces, I'd drop them with a clang into the coffee can I carried along. When I got home, if Dub was out, I'd arrange the pieces on the kitchen table, making a sunshine with sharp green rays or spelling out Dub's name.

When Dub was out at Towne Tavern, I could lounge in the living room, maybe eating spaghetti with red sauce while I watched the game shows. Those were the nights I loved—I felt free, and I pretended the trailer was my own place—that I was living here because I loved it, not because of some silly deal I made six months ago. Those nights I'd take the blue flowered sheets Dub thinks are too girlish and hang them on the window like drapes, like elegance. I'd take pictures from the photo album in my dresser drawer, mostly pictures of me and Carrie taken just before my dad left, tack them up on the panelled wall of the living room, rearrange them, then put them away again. I'd try to feel what it would be like to have a whole trailer to myself, where I could spread out, not be confined to a corner here, a drawer there.

The house I imagine having is pretty much the same as I remember Sarah Tillman's house—a house so strong it smells like me. A house a good man would be drawn to. I think sometimes that it was the house that drew my father away—drew him so quickly to that woman, he forgot his other life. When she was still just a neighbor, my father would take me and Carrie with him for visits, and she'd teach us to split wood, clean tack, or train morning glories up a pole so they didn't spin circles, wrapping around themselves.

But there was one picture I was tempted to leave hanging up—of me, Dad, and Carrie. Mom must have taken it, which I have a hard time remembering, an even harder time believing. It's from one of the few times we went camping down at Moose Jaw Lake. In the picture, Dad's got his arm around me and we're sitting on a picnic table, carving our initials in it. He'd been showing me how to use a jackknife, promising that soon he'd get me one of my own. Carrie's in the background, fishing off a dock, her skinny boy's body in jeans rolled up to her knees, her blonde hair pulled back in a long braid. I'm up front with Dad, my hair red like Mom's, hidden, thankfully, under Dad's cowboy hat. I'd spent a lot of time on that hat, pulling strands from his favorite horses' tails to make a braid that fit around the rim. Cinnamon and Uncle Dean were Dad's favorites, and he could never figure out how I got them to stand still long enough to pull hair for the braid. He kept these horses at Sarah Tillman's. Mom hated horses so she didn't care; by the time I could understand, they'd already moved to Iowa.

I couldn't define what I expected when we got to Massachusetts; I was expecting something so completely new. I knew what I didn't want: I didn't want to live the lives I'd seen played out around me in Blue Earth County. I wanted kids, but I didn't want to be shacked up like Carrie, pregnant by a man who considered a commitment sleeping with only one girl at a time. But maybe what I wanted, more than independence, more than freedom from Webster's Crossing, was a reason. A reason to keep waking up and moving through life.

I loved my mother, in a way I couldn't respect. I didn't want to be thirty-eight and so worried about fitting into my skin-tight jeans that I couldn't eat a chocolate donut. Growing up, she gave me little advice. But I remember what she said when I was thirteen, the year she told me I could smoke in the house if I wanted to, even though I didn't smoke. It was a humid summer evening. Carrie and I sat around the picnic table with Mom while Number Three (I think his name was Carl) cooked up red hots over the bonfire he had going in our backyard. Mom had wild hair, brown and red with grey streaks by her ears, thick and coarse as a horse's tail. When she leaned back to take a slug from her beer, her face looked larger as her hair fanned out behind her neck.

When she straightened back up, she looked right at me and smiled the way she did when she got off work at the plant and was getting ready to go to Margaret's for Buffalo wings and draft beers.

"I've been meaning to tell you a secret," she said, leaning her thin shoulders towards me, the sequins on her black tee shirt catching the light of the fire. She ran her finger around the rim of her Bud bottle. "About religion."

This caught Number Three's attention, and he dropped the stick he'd been poking the fire with and stood at the edge of the table.

"About getting to heaven." She wiggled her head as she smirked, and I could tell she was in the mood to tell a story. So she told us how Grandma was a fundamentalist and a frontierswoman, which I'd heard before. She paused in the right places and Number Three laughed. Carrie and I just sat and listened. When she got near the end, she turned back toward us.

"But I've got my own theory." She was smirking again, holding up her Bud bottle to catch the light of the fire, as if she was about to release some holy wisdom on us. "The only way to get to heaven," she said, "is a tall cool one every night." She burst out with a laugh, though Carrie and I were silent. "Then maybe have a beer afterwards!"

She laughed again while Number Three picked her up and hoisted her over his shoulder like a sack of flour, parading her around the yard as he smacked her butt and she tried to pour beer over his head.

I took a cigarette out of Mom's pack then and lit it, pulling smoke into my mouth and blowing it back out. Carrie's eyes were as wide as quarters, and she kept whispering my name, "Ellen... Ellen," as if I'd forgotten my place. I tried to keep my coughs silent. After a minute Carrie was quiet, and then she took one for herself.

There are two things that stand out to me since we moved here, things that took me awhile to realize, but that differentiate where I am now from where I was. I realized how quickly things bloom here. At home, we didn't have our Apple Blossom Parade until the end of May, while here it seems the apples are just about up and ready by then. It's an exaggeration, but still, it happens. Somehow, I miss things. Like the magnolias here are open in April, and by the time I'm ready for them in May, I've missed my chance.

The other thing I realized was that people are the same. It seems as if you could just take the people from Webster's Crossing—Sampson and Dirk and Sue—and drop them here on the coast, give them new names, make them construction instead of plant workers. Call it Towne Tavern instead of Margaret's. We rediscovered what we'd been meaning to leave.

And lately I have a hard time coming home. The new names are Ricko and Tom, and when I get home, they're already drinking with Dub. Sometimes Stacy is there, too, and she always gives me a dirty look, even though it's my place. They play Flip Jack, a card game they'd made up themselves that has to do with drinking and tens. I go to the bedroom—the only room besides the bathroom with a door—and I flop down on the bed, try to figure out what made me decide it was such a good idea to move out to Massachusetts with Dub McFarlan.

Stacy always smiles at me a moment before we speak, her lips honeymoon red, pulled tight in a grin. The smiles she gives Dub are wide and teethy, accompanied by giggles Tom either doesn't understand or chooses to ignore.

"So," she said once, glancing down casually at my flannel shirt, then meeting my eyes again. "How's the job." It wasn't really a question.

The truth was I loved my job babysitting for a young couple on the other side of town. The kids were a boy and girl, just like I wanted someday. The parents paid me as well as they could, which wasn't much, but they supplemented my pay with dented cans of food they couldn't sell at the Food Lion, where he managed the deli. But Stacy judged you by the magnitude with which you hated your job. And while there was a part of me that would like to not care what she thought, she was the only female I knew in Clarke County, and the closest thing I had to a friend.

"Oh, you know," I said. "It sucks. The kids are brats. The pay's crappy."

"Oh," she said, putting on a pout, her lips pursed as though she was about to kiss, her arms folded across her black knit top, which showed her belly button. Her jeans were white and barely reached her hips. She wore white hoop earrings to match her jeans, and they stood out like day against the thick brown hair she wore curled, then teased.

She brushed her hair over her shoulder. "I keep telling you, you should come work at the salon."

I nodded. The "salon." Like it was French.

"Not that I don't talk about quitting." She pulled a cigarette from her pack of 100s. "Caroline's a bitch." She held the cigarette between her lips and lit it. "I'm just staying there till I get a customer base. Then I'm going off on my own." She took a long drag and pushed smoke out her nose. "Caroline's making a killing on rent for those chairs, especially now that almost half my customers are requests."

I didn't exactly know what she meant but nodded anyway. Though my mother was no saint, one thing she taught me is about other women: the stereotype about cat fights didn't just give birth to itself. There were women it was just better to skirt around, stroke their egos a bit so it didn't come to a contest.

So I told Stacy I was thinking about it. That I'd actually been thinking about a career. What I was doing was no career, and I thought I'd like a career. And the truth was, it sounded good. Not necessarily hairdressing, but something to work at, something to achieve. Stacy smiled again, but this time looked at my face, not at my flannel.

"Oh my God, yes," she said, setting her cigarette in the filled ashtray. "I may knock it. But Caroline's is a great place to begin." She reached over and lifted some of my hair, on the side, then around the back.

I let her touch my hair because it reminded me of when Carrie used to French braid my hair before school. It wasn't just that she brushed back my hair, but that she focused on me.

"You know," Stacy said, leaning back on the kitchen counter, reaching again for her cigarette, "you could take those night courses at the high school. It only takes five months to get certified, and heck, you've already been here for two."

So we planned it all out, how I'd keep the sitting job until I got my certification, then start at the salon by sub-renting her chair on Monday nights, which were the slowest, then working up to Friday lunch. We planned and planned until we had our own shop, until we had ten chairs, two for us and eight we'd rent out. Mostly I kept nodding because the attention felt good; it felt good to plan.

■ ■ ■

Three months had passed since that night Stacy and I sat up talking. By the time I was halfway down Miller Avenue, where the street had solid yellow lines down the middle and streetlights dotting the way, I realized I didn't know what I should do. I could talk Dub into coming home with me, try to get him to walk off his drunk, then snuggle into bed under his dead-weight arm across my chest. Tomorrow morning maybe take out the canoe, maybe show him my glass. And then what?

Once when I was in a high school communications class, we had to split up into groups where we were given lists of one hundred descriptive words. From these lists, we had to choose a word to describe the others in the group. Some were told words like "creative" or "independent" or "pretty." While the word I had imagined for myself was "able," the words chosen for me were "quiet" and "shy." Except by one girl. "I see you as 'regular,'" she said. The group was silent for a moment, and I looked down at my list to stop the rush of tears I felt pushing against my eyes. And there it was, right above "reliable" and "risk-taker." The girl shrugged her shoulders.

Just ahead I could see a shape under the streetlight, slumped on the shoulder of the road. I got closer and saw it was a retriever, his black coat still sleek like mink, his body not arched, not contorted, but sleeplike. The kind of dog so loyal he even died well. I stooped to pet him and I smoothed down his ears as if he was asleep by a fireplace on a thick padded rug. His body was not yet cold, and I suddenly remembered Moonshine, the dog my father bought for hunting just before he left. The dog, too, he kept at Sarah Tillman's. He had brought me along to pick from the litter, and I chose Moonshine because he sat on the outskirts of play, waiting, it seemed, to be held. I knew my father and Moonshine and the horses and Sarah Tillman lived seven states away now, but the thought of them, the thought of this dog on the side of the road, sent me running the rest of the way to Towne Tavern, running for Dub.

It was a large place, with pool tables in the back, mounted fish above the bar. The bouncer let me in when I pleaded and explained I was only there to give Dub McFarlan a ride home. He didn't realize I had no car. A group of girls, in tight jeans and fuzzy pastel sweaters, choking on cigarettes, sat at a round table near the door, which was wide open in the cold November air to let out smoke. They looked up and quieted as I entered, and I overheard Dub's name, but not mine. They didn't know mine.

He was sitting at the far corner of the bar with a draft beer. Ricko saw me first and jerked his chin towards me to warn Dub. Watching Dub's lean shoulders, the way even his chin looked strong as he talked, I remembered how we were at first, a year ago back in Blue Earth County, when he told me one day he wanted to build me a cabin from trees he logged on his own land.

"Dub," I said, and the group of guys sitting near him started to cluck, whistle. "Dub," I said again. "It's time to go."

Perhaps I should have said something more inspiring, something that wouldn't have made me a caricature for them all to hoot about later. But it was all I could think to say.

He ordered another beer as though I wasn't standing there. I couldn't help thinking that my life might be different if I could just walk past those girls, if I just walked the four miles back to the trailer, gathered my plants and my clothes, and called a taxi. But I didn't leave, and when I told him what I'd seen, when I told him about Moonshine, he laughed at me. I slugged him like nothing I knew.

Never having hit anything before, it surprised me how hard his face was, and I knew instantly that my knuckle was worse off than his cheek. In a swift move, Dub grabbed both my wrists in his hands and watched me as I fought with my feet, my knees, smashing him with my hips and shoulders.

The bar was silent and I didn't scream, didn't notice the faces of people circled around us, could only hear the grunts escaping from my throat as though they were someone else's. As I slowed my struggle, Dub asked, "Are you through?"

■ ■ ■

As I walked home from Towne Tavern, I suddenly heard footsteps behind me and knew it was Dub, knew instinctively that if I ran, he'd catch me. For a moment I felt good knowing that as fast or as far as I could go, there'd always be one person who could bring me back. I thought of myself as Sarah Tillman, a woman so strong she could get a man to chase her until he flitted around her like a moth caught in a light.

The footsteps behind me were steady, secure in their strength. He knew he was taller than I was, stronger, quicker. He knew that I'd come there looking for him and now here he was, ready to catch me, to catch me and hold me quick to his love.

Maybe that's why Sarah Tillman ran—the thrill of being chased clear across the state by a desire fierce enough to rip you up by your roots like a tree, your limbs green and so newly exposed to the wind they shiver and hide. I wondered what Sarah Tillman's new house, the house she shared with my dad, smelled like, whether she still kept the wood she split herself on the back porch, whether her hunting bow was in the corner by the fireplace.

Suddenly I no longer wanted to be caught; I wanted to push my legs as hard as they'd known and run till I was half-dead with breath. I slowed my pace slightly, pretending to look around at the stars that littered the sky just so he wouldn't suspect me. The footsteps behind me slowed, relaxed. When I got just beyond the final streetlight, as my eyes adjusted to the newly darkened night, I swallowed hard, whispered "please," a prayer, I don't know to whom, then took off with all the strength I could muster. I got in maybe two or three strides before I heard pounding on the gravel behind me. I pushed with everything I owned, instantly out of breath from the adrenaline racking through my body, shaking my limbs as I ran. He wouldn't let up. I had no idea why he wanted me. It scared me that even though I ran as fast as I could, he could still catch me. I felt his hands on my shoulders, tumbling us both into the ditch.

He landed on top of me and for a moment didn't move. I felt the dry grass on my cheek, the rock that had slammed into my back. He lay still, and I was afraid he would kiss me, could feel his breath, musty with beer, in short gasps on my cheek. In the moon's light, I could see his cheek swelling where I'd hit him, his hair in long strands over closed eyes. When he opened them, I turned away, and he did the same. He got up without helping me, climbed out of the ditch. We walked slowly, and I was just behind him, and though he didn't say anything, I sensed he wanted to. I didn't quicken my pace to match his stride.

I noticed small glints of glass in the gravel. I picked them up piece by piece, putting them in my pocket, ignoring the tiny cuts they made on the tips of my fingers. I thought maybe I'd leave him my collection, though I would never find out what he could have seen in it. When I started walking again, he was a quarter-mile ahead. He was still walking more slowly than his normal pace, but now with his shoulders slumped and his hands in his pockets, like he walked when we used to hike through the trails by Cisco Bay, not tall and stiff like when he was out. As I got closer to the place where the dog had been, I looked for it, looked in the ditch, then on the other side of the road. As I walked past that spot, I knew he was gone, and I thought maybe he had never been there.

UNTITLED   6" x 9"   **STACEY DRESSEN-MCQUEEN**
acrylic & ink on glass

I paint small prayers to myself. I work to give myself a sense of place and inner time. The scraping and scratching and building up in the process of reverse glass painting is very satisfying. I like to give my pieces a sense of being worn and patched.

UNTITLED 6" x 9" **STACEY DRESSEN-MCQUEEN**
acrylic & ink on glass

The Floating Sari

Whenever I thought of her, two images came to mind: a sky-blue sari softly billowing on the river's green surface, mirroring dying ripples, and brown breasts as plump as raisins, as solid as eggplants, resting on a swollen belly creased with yellow stretch marks like the markings on watermelons. As we reclined on the porch, our backs on the sun-warmed wood, she would patiently explain which child had suckled which breast.

These memories are from long ago when she was another woman, someone who used her bulk to push her husband around when money to buy groceries somehow found itself paying for gin, someone who toiled daylong under the blistering tropical sun because her only skills lay in her hands. The old woman learned how to help things grow by caring for numerous infant cousins after her parents took her out of school in her third year. Help was needed and girls didn't require education. In this way she acquired a talent for nurturing that she used to coax rows of curly runner beans and vines of passion fruit from the hard Fijian soil. Later, when she moved to Canada, she would boast to her cronies how an uneducated Indian woman managed to get all her children educated.

When it came time for our weekly chat, I decided to ask her about my dream, which had recurred frequently when I was growing up, forcing me awake, drenched in sweat.

"Hello, *bhuria*," I teased, knowing that calling her "old woman" would pique her vanity.

"Old woman. Who's the old woman? I've had eight children and I'm not the one who takes naps in the afternoon."

"Hey, you called on Saturday afternoon during prime nap time. I just need more sleep these days." Recently, whenever she called, I could be found dozing in the warmth of my lumpy sofa. "Oh, I meant to ask you: Do you remember that time you almost drowned? I dreamt about it again. You were standing by the water, dressed in your favorite sari, a sky blue. It floated around you as you broke through the surface of the water. Do you remember?"

"*Neh betti,* I don't remember," she said, her voice barely audible. "When did it happen?"

"I was three or four years old, and it was a hot day. I cried for a long time, not knowing you could swim. You must remember something."

"Oh, yes, yes, I do. Where did you say it was? You were such a little girl, always a few steps by me. How could you know what happened then?"

"I thought I'd lost you and ever since, I dream of that floating blue sari. What happened that day?"

"Why are you wasting your money talking about this long distance? Come up and see me and we'll talk about it then, *yaar,*" she said, her voice growing faint. "Anyway, I don't remember. Drink a glass of cold water before bed and it'll empty out the bad dreams."

She sounded tired so I decided not to push her. I promised myself that I'd bring it up when I saw her next. We talked for a little while longer, catching up on a week's worth of news, teasing each other affectionately. It was the only way I knew to force her out of the glum reverie that clung to her in that empty house.

I say empty, but that's not quite true. Excitable grandchildren stayed with her after school as she bustled, alternately scolding them and preparing cups of hot milk laced with cinnamon and *roti* slathered with butter and jam. And of course there was her husband, squeezed onto the end of the sofa opposite her, offering the sum of his concentration to game shows and soap operas.

An unspoken competition for space existed between the two—the chattering of her wide-band radio with its perpetual rounds of "Hindi Hits" fought the constant drone of the TV. Married at the age of fourteen, they continued the centuries-old tradition of an elaborate distance between an Indian husband and wife. Neither knew how to show affection to the other—if it was there. The buffer of grandchildren saved them from ever learning about one another.

"*Yaar,* it's very cold here, I can feel it in my bones," she said. "And my marigolds are dying. I can't go outside to water them now. That stairway frightens me. Of course, nobody else here can water my flowers," she sniffed.

I wondered what he had done to piss her off this time. It was always about something more, that was the Indian woman's way—to confront a problem by circling around it. A comment about the salt in the rice might mask a rage waiting to explode in sobbing fits and bitter words spat out until the early hours.

"I'll come up next weekend and help you water the marigolds. Do you need anything from here?"

"*Cochnai lhurki*, I don't need anything. Are you coming with Ghura?"

"His name is Gary. Gary. He's not a horse, for heaven's sake. Why do you have to make his name sound Indian?"

"Ghura, Pura, Bura. What's the difference? How is he?"

"Fine. But I'll be coming alone."

We discussed the time of my arrival and I pried a wish list out of her: low-salt butter to make *ghee*, dried black-eyed peas for mouth-watering curries, and canned pink salmon, which costs more in Canada. She believed America bulged with cheap foodstuffs and constantly inquired about the price of egg-plant, flour, okra, and milk. The thought of abundance pleased her, so when-ever I visited, I loaded up on her favorite items and anything else I could le-gally drive into Canada.

These were my little gifts for the hospitality shown towards Gary, who, upon entering her house, was asked if he cared for a piece of Indian sweet, a bite of chicken curry, a pillow to rest on, or a cup of the hot tannin-rich bitter tea they favored. It always amused me to think about how the generosity of Indi-ans extended more readily to outsiders than toward family members. But the old woman was sincere in her generosity.

That night as I curled up against Gary's warm body, I thought back to three years ago when I finally left home after twenty-five years. An opening in the Seattle office of the accounting company where I worked lured me to the States. I met Gary at a benefit for a local theater company that I was auditing. He en-tered my life lightly, quietly, moving with the grace and hidden strength of the dancer he was. Life alone in the cocooning warmth of my studio apartment suited me. But Gary held himself with a stillness borne of knowing how far he could extend himself. That appealed to me. His presence didn't drown me.

I rubbed my toes against the thick veins scrawled above his ankle bone and gently elbowed him awake.

"Gary, I'm going up to Vancouver this weekend."

"Alone?" He was instantly awake. His eyes were deep and black, as black as mine. I rolled onto him and smiled, brushing my lips against the angles of his cheeks and jaw. The heat between us burned my flesh as I moved against the muscles of his thighs, marveling at his pleasure.

"I'm going to tell them why I've needed so much sleep lately."

He pursed his lips in concentration, not saying anything for a couple of minutes.

"Sure you want to do it alone?" he finally asked.

That was kind of him. Just over a year ago, I finally got around to telling them about my new boyfriend but neglected to mention he was African American. Gary's silence when I first brought up the topic of dark-skin prejudice among Indians, and our endless discussions afterwards, convinced me that the element of surprise would be the best way to handle the situation. I was counting on the deeply ingrained concept of hospitality that centuries of karma-tending had imprinted on Hindus.

Gary's first visit was difficult for us. Since I considered myself independent and strong, even a bit of a rebel, it surprised me to realize how much it mattered what the old woman thought about him. It quickly became apparent that my guerrilla tactics were going to be handled politely, as was Gary. They lavished the same kind of attention on him that they would on any stranger to their home. Gary wore their solicitations well. How was he to know that moving in with an Indian woman meant moving in with her entire family? The family was always there—an invisible presence wedged between the daughter and the outsider. It didn't strike me till I left home, but individual and collective space are indistinguishable among Indians of a certain generation, who feel they have a right to determine their relatives' lives. It's like having my family and every generation before them crowd around me until there isn't any room to breathe.

"I'll go up first and tell them we're expecting a baby. If the prospect of a dark grandchild doesn't kill them, then the fact that we're living together unmarried just might. You could come up if they take it well, but I don't see why you should have to be there if things get ugly." His arms circled my body, pulling me closer. "You know how much the opinion of their Indian cronies means to them. God knows she wouldn't have stuck it out with my father if she didn't think they'd label her a *bad* woman." I waited for him to say something. He traced my spine with a finger, lazily moving down the length on my back.

"It's our baby, Manju, and I'd like to be with you on this. God, let's not go over this again. I'll come up the next day regardless of the welcome you receive, but you tell them first, if it helps you. Just no surprises, okay?"

■ ■ ■

The Vancouver sky hung sullenly over the stucco house as I turned the key. I stood in the doorway inhaling the scent of *garam marsala,* garlic, and oil, the smells of an Indian home washing over me in a flood of memories. She had been waiting all morning for my dusty Honda to turn into the driveway. My boots joined the assembly of shoes lining the entryway and I padded up the stairs. As usual, she was seated on the ratty brown sofa, ready for me. The scent of Pond's cold cream clung to her cheeks. I gave the old man a quick peck on the cheek. It always surprised me when they didn't recoil from my demonstrations of affection. Maybe they attributed it to the influence of a Canadian education on my upbringing. The old woman smiled and motioned for me to sit beside her.

"You look fat," she said, examining my rounded hips and belly.

"Well, thanks a lot. I didn't drive all the way up here just to get insulted."

She laughed, the afternoon light catching the gold fillings between her teeth. I settled into the rituals of my visits: the old woman gripped my hand while, across the room, he asked detailed questions about gas mileage, line-ups at the Canadian-U.S. border, and traffic on the way to Vancouver. After a while, he returned to the hockey game on TV and she and I ambled to the kitchen to check on cumin-laden scents wafting from the curries. She always cooked my favorite dishes, knowing quite well that I lacked patience for the elaborate preparations and the constant watching required to ensure a curry thick with the blended flavor of garlic, oil, spices, and gustatory lust (the only kind a good Indian woman should have).

After checking the steaming pots on the stove, she surprised me by handing over two plump mangoes and asking me to prepare a chutney to accompany the lamb curry. To humor her, I carefully grated the mangoes into the shredded cilantro and garlic mixture.

"Mix it well. Put in more salt," she scolded over my shoulder. "I don't know why you never salt your food enough. Your curries will lack a good body and will never be tasty. Then who'll come to eat at your house?"

I smiled and continued to mix it my way.

After dinner, we rested on her bed, another ritual. She liked to eat but was sometimes seduced too much by the food. A little rest after dinner allowed the last forced bites to digest. Although my mother was relatively young, lack of adequate health care for pregnant women in a poor country took its toll on her health. Sometimes it helped ease the aches if I walked on her back. But tonight, she wanted a scalp massage and settled herself on the floor with her back pressed against the edge of the bed while I rubbed coconut oil on my hands in preparation. To help pass the time, I asked her for a story. She loved to talk about her village days and would spin stories of murder and abductions. With a shawl wrapped over her shoulders, head tilted back on my lap, eyes closed tight with memories, she let the words stream out in a sing-song voice. She told me she had a new story, the story of Lali, a prostitute's daughter, who could only look forward to the craft of her mother.

"Why couldn't she do something else?" I asked.

"What else, *yaar!* She had no dowry, her mother was a bad woman, and she lived with prostitutes. Just listen to my story."

■ ■ ■

Lali shivered as she neared the window, the noonday sun shimmering with the heat below. A breeze played on her naked body, raising little brown goose bumps along her arms and legs. She stood on the ledge and waited. Like unwanted relatives who arrive without notice, her destiny closed in unerringly. A buzzing crowd gathered three stories below her and women in bright saris shifted their children more comfortably on their hips as they gawked at the sight of Lali swaying.

"Aray, larhki, conchi, cartha?" called out a wizened old woman from the crowd. Lali's starving brown body stood in stark contrast to the peeling white-wash of the Lakshmi Mercantile Building. She gently bent her knees, raised her hands, turned, and let all one hundred pounds of her body fall forward. Later, the women in the market could not remember exactly what happened. Terrible memories are like that. They only remembered the sound of a collective gasp and their heartbeats thundering in their ears. It was lucky for Lali that Motti Bhayni squatted below with her cotton saris laid out in candy-colored mounds. Lali landed on both the saris and Motti Bhayni.

She was told all this later, when her baby was due. She only remembered the whispering against her face, her body plunging into nothing...then, hitting hard against twin pillows of flesh. That was also the only time she dared open her eyes. Her head had rested against the enormous breasts spilling out of Motti Bhayni's kurta. It had been a fateful meeting for the women. Motti took pity on the thin girl and decided to take Lali home, and when the time came, she helped her through a difficult birth. The hips of a tiny thirteen-year-old weren't quite ready for an eight-pound baby.

They easily identified the father from the little girl's features. He was a regular customer at the house Lali lived in with her mother and ten other women, all of them indentured prostitutes. Late one night, the man mistakenly entered Lali's room and, drunk with whiskey and the anticipation of compliant flesh, proceeded to pound his body into the struggling Lali whose screams were smothered by thick fingers thrust into her mouth.

Lali lived with Motti and learned to sell saris. After Motti grew disinclined to perspire under the heat of the midday sun, Lali took over the business.

■ ■ ■

"So what did people say about her baby?"

"Nothing. What could they say? She expanded the business and bought the stall run by Bisun, who sold tender *samosas* and hot, sweet *chai*. He was a good man. They became friends and he stayed to cook for her. And, for the rest of her life, Lali's stomach was full."

I wondered if this was the right time, clutching the edge of her shawl, which was decorated with trailing elephants, each trunk entwined with the tail of the preceding animal. I swallowed my nervousness.

"*Umma*, do you remember that dream I talked about on the phone?"

She opened her eyes slowly and flexed her neck to stretch out the kinks. I helped her as she grunted off the floor.

"I've forgotten so many things about Fiji, especially back when you were young. Fiji is just a memory now of a place that seems far away. Why is this dream important to you?"

"I don't know. Sometimes I wonder if any of it ever happened. Maybe I made it up. Maybe that's all it is, a dream. It's hard to block out the sight of the blue sari and your hair spread out on the water. I didn't think you'd ever surface."

She cocked her head and slowly walked towards the altar in her closet. Every Friday morning after cleansing herself thoroughly, she would light incense and pray to Lakshmi, the goddess of fortune. Her face looked closed and distant, as if her thoughts were miles away. This wasn't going as I planned and I regretted not having Gary there to help me. He may not understand Hindi, but he kne. how to read the hidden signs of body language. I suddenly found my body turning rigid with tension. She turned to face me.

"Give me some money—a dollar coin is enough. Next Friday, I'll light an incense for the baby."

I gasped, wondering how she knew. She laughed at my expression, shuffled back to the bed, and reached for my hands.

"Why else are you sleeping so much and getting fat? I grew up in a village where every young girl's posture was examined to see if she was carrying a child. It's a good thing to have lots of grandchildren."

A wonderful sense of lightness swept through me, and I threw my arms around the old woman while she protested about squeezing too tight and hurting the baby.

That night, exhausted from the emotions of the last couple of days, I fell into a heavy sleep. It was the last time I ever dreamt of myself crying on the edge of the riverbank, watching my mother drift away.

SALOME   24" x 18"   **NICOLE M. RAWLINS**
                          etching

It is my intent to create, through my artwork, my own mythology/storytelling of the feminine experience—one that reveals truths about our emotions, psychology, beliefs, sexuality, and growth. Through the manipulation of the media, and through historical, architectural, literary, and dance/performance references, this inner drama is played out.

KELLY 20" x 16" **ALEX ZAPHIRIS**
silver b&w print

This photo is part of a project that tries to capture women's experiences of their homes, and it reflects my own evolving sense of home. The women in these photographs are not simply "models." Each has made important contributions to the creative process. In this collaboration, each woman identified an aspect of "home" that for her was most salient, helped with composition, and reviewed final prints.

Small Stones

for my sister

You jumped off swings in midair,
coasted down the driveway standing on the seat
of your tricycle. Once you ran
into a hammock frame, eye level,
and the neighbor held your bloody face
in her apron. I was proud of your trips
to the Emergency Room.
I envied your broken bones.

I was the quiet one, reading ten books a week.
Only once I hung from the monkey bars,
swinging until the boys' gym teacher
asked if I had permission,
and told me that I must swallow
four small stones in punishment.
A man's palm could fit around my shin—
but I wanted to be even smaller.

I do not want to remember
when you were afraid

of the ice-cream vendor, who insisted
he could not pronounce his own last name,
who wanted to take you
into the back alley.
I do not want to remember the doctors
at the hospital who suggested tranquilizers,

worse than pebbles.
I think of tranquilizer guns,
the lean rifles aimed at animals wandering
in the wrong place. The man saying:
You are dangerous.
I will put you to sleep,
release you stiff and dizzy
in a strange place.

growth

don't hit me, my sister said.
while I danced on water
I was immune, you see.
I only felt him as a caress.
he was like a god to me.
I would hold his vibrant body
as he slammed me down.

she screamed at me,
called me to come to her
but the waters cooled me down,
made me forget.
the cleansing pond
slowly grew stagnant
and I asked him to
come swim with me.

I could see, strangely, clearly
through the waters of
algal blooms and bottom-feeding fish.
for the first time,

I felt his kisses as blows
and I felt him hold me under
as the water filled my mouth
and nostrils and choked me.

at the last moment I saw her.
she was standing by watching me.
my years of ignorance had taught
her the same. her eyes watching
and filling her body with masturbation
as my drowning body and his power
turned her on; and as I had before,
she walked on water, her body flying.

For My Sister at 17

I
She dances the fight,
a drill dance.
She kicks through the living room
and menaces the empty chairs,
prepares to test for the last belt.

They're colored for the damage, she says:
white is harmless, yellow for scrapes,
blue for bruises, red for blood, black for death.

Tomorrow she will dance opponents,
strong men. Masters will watch.
They will decide the warning on her waist.

II
She blacks her combat boots on the kitchen table.
Inspection tomorrow, she says.
I can make Superior Cadet of the Year.
Nobody's boots shine like mine.

She knows a trick our father taught her,
daubs lighter fluid
over a thick-smeared layer of black,
holds a flame to it—a moment of heat and dull light.

She smoothes the steaming melted mass
and works a transformation.
They do shine.
I can see the kitchen, myself, her face, her hands,
in a reflection folded around that shape.

III
In combat-cotton olive drab
blotched with leaf light,
she loads her pack
for a three-day trial in the field:
flashlight, compass, knife.

She opens the door
and runs into the garden
laughing, singsong,
I'm all camouflaged,
you can't see me.

She steps into the shadow
of the yew tree
and vanishes.

KRAKOW, 1994   10" x 8"   **REBECCA HOLDEN**
b&w photo

I have begun to believe in the superstition that when I take someone's photograph, I steal their soul. This doesn't mean that I see myself as a version of the devil, but that I see my photographs as more than just pictures, more than simple records of passing moments.

ANNIVERSARY 10" x 8" **REBECCA HOLDEN**
b&w photo

A successful image for me is one that tells the viewer something about the person or place that normally lies beneath the surface. In other words, the image should go deeper than a postcard or, for example, a high school senior's studio photograph. It should capture a feeling, a personality, a bit of soul.

The Front Lines

The building is not there. I get off the train, cross two streets, and don't see the Planned Parenthood clinic. Instead, I see charred stumps of lumber and a few bent I-beams. What was once the clinic is now a blackened wreck. Beside it is the Veteran's Aid Office—still recognizable, but with a huge hole in its main window. Behind me traffic continues, and overhead the northern California sky spans unbroken. It is 8:30 a.m. on the day after Labor Day, 1990, and I have just arrived for my shift in the front office.

People walk through the wreckage, lifting things and letting them drop. They move slowly, with resignation. They are my colleagues and their loved ones, and their faces are smeared with soot.

I take a deep breath and slowly climb what is left of the front stairs. At the top I find Helen, my supervisor, bent over a heap of something that looks melted. When I come up behind her and say her name, she stands and turns around, startled. Her glasses are smudged and her dark hair unbraided.

"Hi Debbie," she says. She notices I am wearing a skirt and blouse. "Didn't you get the call?" she asks. "We were firebombed last night."

■ ■ ■

A few weeks after moving to California with my boyfriend Ben—a year before the bombing—I walked into a Planned Parenthood clinic for my annual ob/gyn exam. The walls and counters were covered with information on reproductive health. I studied the timid, frightened faces of the waiting clients and thought, I know how to teach; I can do something for them.

I volunteered that day, right after my exam. A month later, I started the long training to administer pregnancy tests and counsel clients. I learned to talk to women about their options for conception and prevention, for continuing and terminating pregnancies. I learned to dispense condoms and prenatal vitamins and to make referrals to various agencies and healthcare providers. I learned to use plastic models, drawings, and sometimes no props whatsoever to describe how human reproduction works, and I learned the rudiments of helping physically and mentally disabled women, women who speak little English, homeless women, hostile and desperate women.

■ ■ ■

Helen brushes her sooty hands on her sooty jeans and tells me that someone heaved a brick through the waiting room window last night and fire-bombed the front office. The news makes me dizzy for a moment; the bright sky swims.

"I'm sure someone called," Helen continues. "We must have just missed you."

I nod, staring around. "Was anyone hurt?"

"No," she says. "Jan"—the clinic director—"got a call from the fire department at four this morning and came right over. Penny's here now with a television crew." Penny, the regional director, is resolute and capable. I feel better knowing she's here.

Helen says that the medical areas and some of the counseling rooms are still standing, and that the damage to the medical records hasn't been determined. The underground phone lines are intact.

I ask, "How can I help?"

Helen peers at me through her large, round glasses and asks, "Are you okay?"

I tell her the shock won't hit me for hours. "I'd like to work while I can."

She suggests that I check the basement and tote up spare shelving for whatever supplies and records we have left. She also advises me to call someone to bring me proper work clothes. I close my eyes and stand still for a moment, praying silently.

■ ■ ■

Before being hired here, I volunteered for nine months at two other clinics as a pregnancy counselor. My first client, thirteen years old, came in with her thirteen-year-old boyfriend. I told the girl that I could talk to her alone if she wished, but she declined. With a staffer observing me, I gave them the pregnancy test results, figured out the girl's due date, and evenhandedly stated the options. They agreed that an abortion was best. I watched carefully and saw no coercion or discord. That decided, I explained the procedure and showed them the surgical instruments. Then I launched into a discussion of birth control methods. They hadn't asked for it, but it was my job to give it. They asked good questions and thanked me. I sent them to the front office for scheduling, something volunteers were not legally allowed to do. I spent the remainder of my shift filling out state paperwork, which did not have categories for this sort of case. How could I report a state-funded abortion for a minor without implying the girl had been raped? How could I make sure that the boy didn't get into more trouble than he already had? How could I report that they were minors without involving their parents and the school board too much?

That was one of my easier cases. The hardest was the woman whose husband kept stealing her birth-control pills. After having a private investigator follow her to the clinic, he harassed all of us for information on her case. On the day of her abortion, he came to the clinic drunk and we had to block him from the abortion suite hallway with our bodies.

■ ■ ■

I walk through the wreckage gingerly. Things pop and crunch under my feet. I ignore the television cameras, just wanting to get to the staff room and put my lunch away. I find the small kitchen crowded with brooms, shovels, and vacuum cleaners. I put my bag down in a corner and strip off my blouse, tucking my earrings in the pocket.

I pick up the phone to call Ben. Even though our relationship dissolved four months ago, he still has keys to my car. Our breakup wasn't entirely amicable, but we do intend to be friends. I miss him. He isn't pleased to hear from me, but he agrees to take the bus to my place, pick up the work clothes and tools I need, and drive my car to the clinic.

■ ■ ■

Although we'd once intended to marry, Ben and I broke up a few weeks after I'd been hired. Thereafter, I found myself envying my clients their romantic relationships. I'd listen to a woman describing what she and her lover were doing when the condom fell off, and I'd wish we could talk about something else. One of my most difficult duties in this respect was determining the due date of pregnancies, which I did by using a cardboard "gestation wheel"— the obstetrician's slide-rule. While telling a client how soon she had to decide what to do, I'd involuntarily figure out how long it had been since Ben and I had made love.

Women often sobbed on the phone and in the counseling rooms when I told them they had passed the legal time limit for abortions, that, according to California law, they were now mothers. I could not, however, discuss my own divided life.

■ ■ ■

After the phone call, I head for the basement, a locked storage area with an outdoor staircase. I find Courtney at the top of the stairs. Courtney and I were born on the same date—August 24, 1963—an hour apart, on opposite coasts. We do not look alike, but in times of crisis we think the same way, like identical twins. We're the two physically strongest staff members, so we're both doing the heavy lifting; we're also both wearing skirts. We smile at each other, then go down the stairs.

One of us unlocks and opens the basement door. The other reaches around the doorway and flicks the light switch. We wait outside and listen. We have independently developed the same careful procedure for entering this easy-to-break-into room. There is no sound inside; when we peek around the doorway, everything is where it should be. The cool, dry air flows over us. We glance at each other and enter.

Without speaking, we unload boxes of birth-control pills and sterile gauze pads from the movable steel shelves. When a shelving unit is empty, we lift it between us and set it outside the door. We agree to quit after four units because the floor is getting unnavigable. We turn off the light and lock the door, then carry the units one by one up the stairs, not needing to discuss who should go backwards. When we finish, we hug at the top of the stairs and part ways.

■ ■ ■

When I was hired here, at the highest-volume clinic in our region, I had to decide in which service or services I wanted to work: front office/pregnancy counseling, health care clinic, or abortion clinic. Jan and Helen gave me a few days to think it over. I was already trained in pregnancy counseling and much of the office work, so I knew I would enjoy working there. I realized I had little interest in the health-care clinic, since my duties would be restricted to assisting the nurses, which seemed less interesting than talking to clients. Did I want, then, to work in the abortion service, assisting a doctor, staying with a client throughout the procedure?

Questions burned in my mind for two days. Did I want to help women in crisis? Of course. Did I believe in a woman's right to her own body? Absolutely. Did I feel comfortable about physically assisting in the act of terminating potential lives?

When I told Jan and Helen that I didn't want to work in abortion services, they just nodded and checked off my preference on their hiring forms. "No problem," Jan said. "It's good that you know how you feel. Many of us feel the same way."

■ ■ ■

As I turn at the top of the stairs to go inside, a beat-up, white Oldsmobile pulls up along the sidewalk. This is a common occurrence; people often ask for directions on this block.

The driver, a graying man in a flannel shirt, leans out the window and shouts at me, "You godless whore! I'll pray for you! Jesus saves!"

"I'll pray for you, too!" I shout back. I am trained not to encourage confrontation, but it has been a bad day.

He has already rolled up the window and driven off.

■ ■ ■

Many of my colleagues used to speak ill of religious people. I couldn't blame them: pro-life protesters who identified themselves as Christians marched three days a week outside the clinic, quoting the New Testament and calling us heathen sluts. However, I am an observant Jew raised to be tolerant, so I took care never to put down protesters for their religious beliefs, hoping my colleagues would follow suit. Most did.

I sometimes felt responsible for demonstrating that God and pro-choice sentiments can coexist. I worked just as many hours and just as hard as everyone else, but I avoided Saturday shifts to observe my Sabbath. The worst protest actions usually occurred on Saturdays, so I felt disloyal when I missed them. When counseling clients who had religious concerns about birth control and abortion, however, I had a sense of being in the right place at the right time.

Although the clinic accepted my religious choices, the town did not. Swastikas were common graffiti at the train station I used every day.

■ ■ ■

I squeeze through the dented security doors into the medical area and find Marla, our senior clinician, scrubbing blackened countertops. Her gray hair is peppered with soot.

"Hi, Debbie. Could you take over for a minute while I check the sterilized stuff?"

"Sure."

She unlocks a drawer and pulls two latex gloves out of a box. "You'll need these—there's lots of broken glass."

I put them on, unrolling them up to my wrists. In the exam room, Marla opens the door of the metal supply cabinet and shouts, "The surgical packs are *covered* with soot!" She slams the door closed.

Emerging from the room, she sighs, "Well, we won't be doing surgery any time soon anyway...."

When we wipe the counter with paper towels, the towels turn black and leave the counter black. All our test tubes and tables, microscopes and slides, gauze pads and syringes—everything is contaminated.

■ ■ ■

When the clinic began to do HIV testing, I was too new a volunteer to train for HIV counseling. I helped those being trained by having my blood drawn. Blood has never bothered me, so I didn't mind being interrupted on phone duty to have my sleeve rolled up and my veins poked. The phlebotomist-in-training would wear gloves and a mask and treat my sample as if it were dangerous. Because so many of us worked with blood, our dress code stated that we had to wear closed shoes, even on the hottest days, to prevent injury and possible infection from dropped needles.

■ ■ ■

Helen comes inside while I am cleaning Marla's counters to tell me Ben has arrived. I rush outside and see that his long, brown hair is in disarray and he hasn't shaved for a while. I wonder how he has been, whether his carelessness about shaving means he is depressed. When he turns to me I reach out to hug him. Without hesitating, he puts both arms around me and draws me close, standing still.

I ask if he will stay and help us clean, but he says no. I offer to drive him to his office, but he declines, saying he can see I am needed on site. I know he is too frightened to feel he can help. He thinks he isn't welcome here, like he thought he wasn't welcome in my synagogue, in my activist groups, among my friends.

He touches my hand briefly—his fingernails are bitten down. Then he leaves for the train.

■ ■ ■

Once, during an abortion, a woman almost died on our operating table. She stopped breathing even before we gave her a local anesthetic. Pat barreled through the hallway shouting, "Clear the entrance for EMTs!" so I put down my phone and went out after her, moving chairs and clients aside.

An ambulance arrived in ninety seconds. By that time, the woman had revived. She had no knowledge she'd been dead. Pat told me later that the woman had "a little epilepsy" and didn't see why she should have mentioned it to our medical staff.

Two days later, the pro-life protesters carried signs that read, ANOTHER AMBULANCE, ANOTHER BOTCHED ABORTION.

■ ■ ■

Once I've changed into jeans, Helen assigns me to answer phones. I would rather do physical labor, but no one else is qualified for heavy phone duty. It will certainly be heavy: usually three of us handle five lines. Someone has already called clients to cancel appointments; now someone has to receive incoming calls and refer people to two nearby clinics, which have contacted standby clinicians to handle our client load.

"What will I tell them about why we're closed?" I ask Ruth.

"There's no press release yet," she says. "Don't worry, you'll think of something."

Since the front office is nothing but charcoal and melted plastic, I step into the nearest counseling room. It's dark, it reeks of smoke, and there is nothing inside but a desk. The phone, like all the counseling room phones, has no ringer. A light flashes on its base. I pick up the receiver and punch the lit button.

"Planned Parenthood, this is Debbie. May I help you?"

"Yes, I'm calling to reschedule an appointment for a pap smear today."

"We're having some technical problems right now that prevent me from rescheduling your appointment. Can you call us back tomorrow?"

"Tomorrow?" she says. "Listen miss, I just ran out of pills because your clinic didn't remind me to have an exam—"

"I'm sorry for the inconvenience. At the time of your last exam, I'm sure someone told you we can't afford to send out reminder cards like a gynecologist's office. Let me give you the number of our San Ramon clinic. They've opened up several appointments and will be happy to see you immediately if you tell them you're our client."

"San Ramon? What the hell—? I'll have to cancel my hairdresser—"

There are two more lights flashing. "Excuse me, ma'am. I've got another call coming in. Will you hold?"

I punched another button. "Planned Parenthood, this is Debbie. May I help you?"

A male voice. "Are you the bitches that killed my girlfriend's baby?"

"I'm sorry, we can't give out information on who we see here. I have another call coming in. If you'll hold on I'll be back to help you—"

"You fuckin'—"

I punch the third light. The fourth has started flashing. "Planned Parenthood...."

Someone stops by with a television camera and films me standing in the dark room in my tank top, jeans, and work boots, holding a phone receiver in sooty gloved hands. I don't look up.

■ ■ ■

As a front office worker, I was trained to talk with hostile callers, shy callers, terrified callers, suicidal callers, and homicidal callers. It was my job to make appointments, give referrals, or counsel on the spot. I was to refuse abortions to callers who sounded as if they were being coerced, to callers who sounded even faintly unsure, and to callers other than the client herself. I made a lot of mothers angry by insisting that they hand the phone to their daughters and leave the room, and I infuriated a lot of men by asking them to please hang up and let their girlfriends call me.

I also was to withhold information about anyone who set foot in our clinic, including staffers, for their own safety. Just before I was hired, a staff member at a nearby clinic was murdered in the parking lot by someone who found out her schedule and waited for her to leave at night. I was therefore required to be extremely stubborn—yet courteous—about security over the phone. Last names, schedules, and phone numbers were classified. I had to say, "I'm not authorized to give out that information," and stand by it.

Phone work has its moments, though. My first day on the job, I got a call from a woman who needed instruction on inserting a tampon. I talked her through it, and my coworkers applauded when we finished. Then there was the young man who called wanting a referral to a doctor about a problem he would not describe to me. He kept insisting it was "private." I finally said, "Listen, nobody ever calls Planned Parenthood for anything that *isn't* private!" The staffer training me laughed quietly; the young man relaxed.

■ ■ ■

After about an hour of answering five phone lines, I'm dizzy. I lurch out the doorway through the front office wreckage and get outside, where I drop onto a chair and put my head between my knees. Rowena, a medical assistant, breaks an ampule of ammonia under my nose before I can count four breaths. Her lupus has been acting up lately; she shouldn't be here. She asks me whether I am going to faint; I tell her no. I breathe deeply, then pull a tissue out of my pocket and sneeze. The tissue comes away black.

"Inhaling smoke!" she says. "You're asthmatic, right? What the hell were you doing in there?"

I tell her I was answering phones. She says Paula will take over and I should go home.

"So should you!" I say.

We both snort, attempting laughter. "Hey," she says. "What were you telling the people who called?"

I sit up straight, lift an imaginary phone to my ear, and say, "I'm sorry, but we're having some technical problems right now that prevent me from re-scheduling your appointment."

Rowena laughs, this time for real.

"That's pretty accurate," says another voice. When I turn around, Penny is looking back at me with steady gray eyes. "I'll be on the news at noon, explaining it all. Why don't you go home and rest?"

"Soon," I say. The truth is, I don't want to leave, to go back to my new house full of strangers, to be without Ben, to be alone with the images of the wreckage, the smell of smoke on my clothes, in my hair, in my nostrils. I stand up and go back inside.

■ ■ ■

In addition to maintaining the anonymity of staff members, phone workers also had to protect the confidentiality of client interactions. We prearranged a code name for the clinic to be used if a third party answered the phone when we called to give lab results. When we sent out written information, we were careful to inquire whether the envelope could have our name on it. Our stash of blank envelopes always dwindled quickly.

We were also trained to take notes during phone conversations without writing down a client's name. We shredded the notes after hanging up.

■ ■ ■

Helen sits on the ground next to a blackened wastebasket, sorting through a pile of rubble.

"Can I help?" I ask, squatting down next to her.

She picks up a bright green file folder labeled "BOMB," laughs, and pitches it into the wastebasket.

■ ■ ■

Everyone who answered the phone had to be trained for bomb threats. The "BOMB" folder sat in the front office in an accessible place near one of the phones. It contained several copies of our region's standard form for bomb threats, which asked questions like, Sex of caller? Age? What type of bomb? Where placed? When will it go off? We were supposed to keep callers talking, grab a copy of the form, and scribble down all the information we could get. Although we joked about filling out the form—"Excuse me, sir or madam, would you please tell me what type of bomb you're using? Thanks!"—we took all threats seriously.

We had one evacuation while I was working at the clinic. Andrea, across the room from me, received the call. She stood and waved frantically until someone handed her a bomb form, but the caller hung up before she could get anything useful out of him. The abortion staffers lifted one or two patients into wheelchairs and hurried everyone outside. Front office staff cleared the waiting room, secured the doors and phones—notifying the police and our answering service—and followed. When the police arrived, they and one of our supervisors ransacked the building. No bomb was found. The abortion clinic had to run late that day, which meant that many of our clients couldn't get home by public transportation and that the patients awaiting the doctor at his private practice couldn't see him.

■ ■ ■

I'm quite tired and my breathing is getting more difficult. I consider going home, but I decide to call my friends Ari and Ellen instead, and see if I can invite myself over.

Ari leads services and teaches teenagers at our synagogue. Ellen is an occupational therapist and is over eight months pregnant. They have just moved into a house a few blocks from me, and I spend the occasional Sabbath with them when I feel isolated as the only observant Jew in my house.

I call from the staff phone in the kitchen, leaving a smudge with every key punch. As the phone rings in Berkeley, I pull off my gloves and toss them in the sink. Ari answers.

"I'm so glad you called," he says. "I just saw the story on the news. What's it like there?"

"It's awful!"

"Was that you answering the telephone in the dark?"

"Yes, that was me." Tears start down my cheeks.

Ari asks me please to come over so he and Ellen can feed me dinner. I thank him, wiping my eyes with my bare hands, which come away black.

"D'vorah—" he says, addressing me by my Hebrew name, "—if we have a daughter, we want her to grow up to be like you."

I thank him again. Then I hang up, gather my things, and make my way out of the clinic, stepping carefully.

400 south 5th street

i go to the wrong building
off the bus
across the street
up the stairs.
in the lobby
all the signs are blurred
and sideways
half the arrows lead
down a.hallway housing
only the bathrooms
(the other arrows
point right at me).
when i reach the desk
she looks at me and nods
i finally pull the words
one by one
from under my tongue
i
need
food
stamps

are you on disability?
social security?

have you applied?
are you under eighteen?
are there children in the home?
my no's produce
a small white slip of paper
adult division
main welfare building
400 south 5th street
do you know where that is?
I nod
(i rode past it on the bus
to get to this place)

out the door   up the hill
on the bus   i smell
the perfume of the woman
to my left and the urine
of someone behind me.
a tiny woman in the front
shakes a jug of milky pink liquid
and tells every new rider
she has to drink it all by two
so the hospital people
can take pictures of her insides.
i stare at the pale pale strip of skin
between her white socks
and pink sweatpants.

my hands
turn this address
into tiny shreds of paper

tiny bits of memory of the last time
the back injury
the depressed abusive boyfriend
flunking out of school
the case worker who asked
can't you marry one of your housemates
and get him to pay the bills?

i stare out the dirty window
as we roll past christmas shoppers
gawking at store windows
full of animated mannequins.
in their version
the cinderella in rags
is dressed in rose brocade.

digging through my shame
in search of anger
i find the hunger
that wakes me every other hour
to fill my guts with water
and try to fool my body
just a little longer.
i find the voices of my friends
who remind me, each repeating
you deserve the help you need
stand up to them.
they coax from me the visions
of black-eyed peas and greens
black beans in tortillas
hot beet soup with garlic

and the smile i always wear
when i am cooking
(really cooking)
for myself.

i hold that smile
like a lucky penny in my palm
walk off the bus,
down the street
full of lunch-hour traffic,
new snow
falling between tall buildings.

onions

i wake to the smell of onions on skin, not a crisp, just-cut onion smell, but the old ooze of onion through pores or clinging to fingers after hours of slicing, dicing, chopping. every day for two weeks in cooking school i was assigned the task of chopping fifty pounds of onions into perfect quarter-inch squares. i learned to avoid slicing my fingers. i learned to move quickly and with precision while blinded by tears. i learned to ignore the fact that i was the only person in the class never shifted from onions to carrots, celery, tomatoes. i learned to ignore the comments from the other students about my sex and corresponding needs and weaknesses. i learned to suppress my desire to sink my twelve-inch chef's knife into the belly of the man who whispered repeatedly that he would love to fuck me if i wasn't such a cold bitch. i kept chopping. i stood at the stainless steel table in my white coat and herringbone pants. i ignored the dreams that woke me in cold sweats, reeking of onion.

Melissa Is My Name

So you work at McSomethings.
Slave labour. Cheap teeth.
And the manager says
   "Please make it brief"
says to close up again
"You don't mind
do you"
& you consider stabbing him
with your name tag pin
jab i am not wendy jab i am not wendy jab
i am melissa melissa melissa is my name.
& you step into the black
licorice suck of the parking lot.
fingers grabbing pulling cheap polyester
ripping off your hat,
braids curling out shy underneath
as the slam is softened
and they breathe
"She's a girl" & you are born
into the arms
of the two cops
stuttering sweating sorry sorry sorry.
"We didn't know you were a girl"
& you think how you work all day at school

come home
stick sick food
into the bratty brother that is yours
vacuum cause your mom she's working
for you
for you
you do
homework
one hour
& then it's the burger pit
till midnight
bike home alone
an these guys slinkin slow into the night
don't look back
not knowing you have an ache in your chest;
not knowing you have the word "woman" stolen from somewhere
gleamin cold in your pocket;
& your smile flares into the dark.

Nightshift

When you've worked seven or eight hours
building fireline and cold trailing, and
it's two or three in the morning, then
you just slump down anywhere when
the crew boss lets you break.

At first it's easy to sleep, especially
in the black where the fire's already burned.
The ground retains some of that heat,
and you're still really hot from baking
in the sun and walking over coals.

Once, when we sat down to rest, I fell asleep
with my body propped upright by my line pack,
headlamp still on, lighting up my boots.
The radio woke us finally, stiff with cold and
batteries failing in our lamps.

On really cold nights, it's a lot harder to sleep.
The crews spend time looking for burned-out

stump holes. When we find one, two or three
people rake out any remaining coals and
curl up in the hollow of cooked earth.

I snuggled up against a man from another
crew one night as if he were my brother,
and women who couldn't meet my eyes
during the day gave up their fears for
the more urgent need of staying warm.

We shared our bodies' heat, lying tight as
lovers in a root hole, covered with our gear,
softly telling favorite stories, knotting
our separate experiences into something fragile
that held through the days that followed.

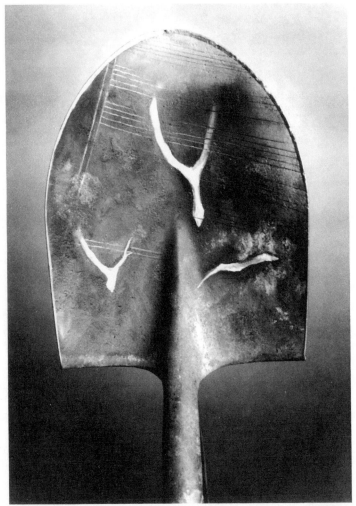

RHYTHM UNBROKEN   **NANCY HAVLICK**

oil paint on shovel head

*This piece is part of a five-part series of oil paint on broken-off shovel heads. The series deals with physical, mental, and spiritual **work**, and with finding a place for the soul through these trials on earth. The series was intended as illustration for an unpublished short story written by a friend.*

GALLON OF MILK   12" x 16"   **MAGDA BAKER**
                          linoleum print

My prints often frame household objects. My work is an exploration of my personal connection to these items and of the paradox of having an emotional attachment to mass-produced things. I both value and resent my connection to the items. They have taught me "femininity," and I value their contribution to my femaleness, but also resent their socially prescribed nature.

Selling Out: Reflections of a Farm Daughter

We both still dream about it. Although it's been nine years since we sold out, my father and I still dream about farming. I dream I am standing in the cow barn waiting for Dad to come home to milk. Dad is running a marathon, but I know that as soon as he's finished he'll come in to start chores and I'm supposed to have everything ready—cows fed and watered, milking machines assembled, udders washed. I look out the barn window waiting for Dad to run by, waiting for the impossible: for my sixty-year-old, 250-pound father to finish running before milking. That's how farming was in the eighties—a perpetual marathon of work, impossible tasks stretched in front of us like miles, undoable in the economic realities of the Reagan years.

Dad wakes from dreaming that the cows haven't been fed in three days. They are dying. He doesn't remember why they haven't been fed, and he doesn't worry that if they haven't been fed, they haven't been milked.

■ ■ ■

The original farm was eighty-seven acres, purchased in 1853 by ancestors immigrating from Vermont. Since then the farm has grown to 220 acres. I often wonder why the immigrants settled in rocky Northeastern Pennsylvania when, if they had moved further south and west, we would have feet of topsoil instead of inches. Locals joke that the land grows only stones naturally. The Vermont immigrants stopped somewhere north of Scranton, Pennsylvania, and south of Binghampton, New York, because land was available, not cleared, barely settled.

Although the growing season was too short and too cold for most things— for example, soy beans are a rarity—the ancestors bought land, cleared it, and began "improving" it: putting up fences with the field stone they cleared, digging wells, raising barns. Well into my father's life the farm was diversified, yielding a variety of products according to the market—chickens, sheep, milk, eggs, butter, pigs, turkeys, and even, in the 1950s and 1960s, Dad's semi-annual crop of beagle puppies.

In 1929 my grandfather began shipping milk to the Dairyman's League, which has since become the Dairylea Milk Cooperative; this began our farm's specialization into a dairy farm. At that point my grandfather had twelve milking cows and shipped forty to sixty gallons (four to six milk cans) of milk a day. When we stopped farming in March 1986, we had around seventy head of cattle, half of them milking cows and the rest young replacement stock, and, if we were doing well, we made about 230 gallons (two thousand pounds) of milk a day. All of the cows were registered Holsteins, born on the farm and raised by us. Although seventy head sounds like a lot to someone who isn't farming, ours was by industry standards a tiny farm, small enough to be worked by one man and his son. Originally it was big enough to support one extended family comfortably, but in the current economy, not viable, not big enough for expensive technology. It was in danger of not producing enough milk to be worth a stop by the milk tankers that transport the milk to the cooperative.

Over the course of my grandfather and father's careers as small farmers, from the Great Depression until 1986, we went from a diversified and largely self-sufficient farm to a strictly dairy-producing farm. There was an increasing pressure to expand and modernize as well as to focus on one product. We kept increasing the number of animals to raise milk production, and we had less and less opportunity to care about individual animals or to care for each other.

■ ■ ■

When I remember how cold it was, I doubt my own recollections. Despite the body heat of seventy animals, it was cold. One-hundred-fifty-year-old barns have no insulation: one layer of boards stands between you and the outside. During the winter, fifty-pound square bales of hay are stacked in the haymow; nothing else protects against the weather, the cold, and the wind chill. The cracks in the walls were as big as my fist. We stuffed them with rags. Frost would form a half-inch layer on the whitewashed walls of the barn. My sisters and I would blow on the frost covering the windows for five minutes to create a space to see out and watch for who would be next to come help.

My sisters and I started helping regularly on the farm when I turned fourteen, in 1982, the year farming got so bad that we could no longer afford a hired hand. We were all growing; we didn't have money for warm coats to wear when we shoveled cow shit or waterproof boots to keep us dry when we watered calves. We had calves tied in every alcove of the barn. We'd haul two twelve-quart, black rubber pails to the thirsty calves, who'd knock against us. The water slopped over our work jeans, down into our old track sneakers. If the calves didn't spill the water, we would undoubtedly knock against a wall in one of the narrow alleyways and dump half the pail ourselves. Once the water spilled, it froze almost instantly, making our jeans like boards—rigid. We had no way to get warm—the only heat source was a small electric space heater hanging in the milk house so the pipes wouldn't freeze.

When I tell people I grew up on a farm, they think my childhood was idyllic, utopian, the great American dream of land and independence. But the reality of farming was brutal and exhausting. I don't want to mask the work, the struggle, the endless battle against government regulations and the inconsistencies of nature with some myth of the salt-of-the-earth farmer, the strong-minded, practical landowner. The problem wasn't the work—the work could be endlessly fulfilling—the problem was the fact that it never stopped. We had no vacations, no time away, no sick leave. A day trip meant milking at four in the morning and driving back by seven for evening milking. When Dad got hurt—and since farming is only slightly safer than coal mining, this happened too often—we had to rely on our neighbors to help us milk until he was able to work again. The cows didn't care if it was Christmas or if someone in the family was in the hospital; the work still needed to be done. But even the endlessness of the labor would have been acceptable, a way of life we all chose together, except that we could not be successful at small-scale farming and we could not expand without incurring tremendous debt. We'd have needed to double the number of cattle and build a new barn with a milking parlor. We couldn't survive economically if we farmed ethically.

Beyond economic considerations, there were the three of us, the farm daughters—who would inherit, who would keep farming? We were all college material—we knew people could farm with a college degree, but school would come first. The other part, of course, was that we were girls, the assumption being that girls and women are not strong enough to farm. Even though much of the work is mechanized and we did help with most aspects of it, we were still girls, and farming was not an option for our future. In college, I researched farm women and found that almost no statistics exist, even though women are often business partners with their husbands. Farm women, and prospects for farm women, remain largely unspoken.

I have two vague memories of why I could not choose to farm. In the first I was with my father when we went to get a part repaired by a local mechanic. They stood in his garage and talked, while I stood in the mud of the mechanic's driveway and played. I had insisted on wearing my black rubber farm boots like my father's and was using them to dig canals and ditches from one mud puddle to another while they chatted. The mechanic looked at me suddenly and said, "I thought only boys liked to play in the mud," and I realized that I was not doing what I was supposed to be doing; I was not where I was supposed to be.

I am less sure of the second memory. I could have made it up, daydreaming, in order to explain conversations I overheard growing up. In this memory the Philadelphia cousins were visiting. They were standing behind the cows, watching Dad milk. I was in front of the cows, pushing hay at them or playing with a calf. The Philadelphia cousins wanted land from the original eighty-seven acres because that land would be inherited by us girls. The Philadelphia cousins were concerned that, after a hundred years, the land would no longer be in the "Green" name. I had to ask my grandmother what they meant by keeping the land in the "Green" name. And when she told me, I decided never to marry, never to have the land's name change. My grandmother and mother hoped I would grow out of this, but I knew then, as I know now, that my name is the only proof I have of belonging on that land.

■ ■ ■

Farming is unpredictable. Small-scale farming, as we farmed, was particularly unpredictable. Resources were scarce; we bought as little as possible and held onto equipment until it was on its last leg. We, like other working-class people, were good at improvisation, imagining, and dreaming the temporary fix. Sometimes it got so cold that the drinking troughs in front of the cows froze, and we had an emergency that required all of us to fix it. The three of us were in the barn with Dad thawing pipes, hauling pails of hot water to the place where the pipes had frozen, throwing rags into the water, and wrapping them onto the frozen pipes with our bare hands. We waited, pressing down on the frozen trough levers, hoping that water would spurt, hoping that we wouldn't have to get more hot water and try again. One Christmas it was so cold that Dad brought a torpedo space heater—a three-foot-long torpedo of blue metal that blasts heat out both ends—into the barn. We stuck it behind the cows in the main barn, ran it five minutes every half hour and watched as the thermometer in the barn rose above freezing during those precious moments of warmth. Running that heater was like prayer. Please God don't let the barn freeze, please God don't let the barn catch fire. A rock and a hard place.

When I look back at the articles I clipped when we were farming, I am amazed at how quickly we sold out. In March 1985 my sisters and father and I were recognized in the local farm magazine, *The Dairy News,* for the century our family had spent farming. In the picture, we hold the original deed to the farm, we smile and display a pile of ribbons won at the local fair. I'm standing with a calf I raised, that I'll show at next year's fair. A year later, all the animals were sold; we were ex-farmers, and my father had a job that meant eight hours a day and benefits.

While we were farming, we had successfully developed our herd of registered Holsteins, improving both milk production and the conformation of the animals. We often won prizes at local fairs and 4-H shows for the quality of the animals. This was the part of farming that most interested me, the genetics—half science, half guesswork—of trying to breed the best producing milk cow with the best conformation. It was also the part of farming that was most acceptable for me to be good at as a girl. I loved taking care of the young stock, and I loved reading the bull catalogues and matching bulls with cows, trying to imagine what the herd would look like in the future.

When my first 4-H animal was born, I knew before she hit the ground that if she was a heifer, she would be my champion show cow. My father and I worked it out. This mythic calf was the granddaughter of our best cow ever, a cow that classified as an excellent 90. I had known the mother, Nancy, since she was born. She was a big, skinny, raw-boned, mostly white cow—a pretty good milker, reliable, calm. Nancy was bred to an Elevation son, a good bull, one that should have done something for the calf's conformation. We hoped that the calf would be a champion like her grandmother and that good traits tended to skip a generation. We also hoped that Nancy wouldn't have a bull calf, because then he would be sold for veal within a week of his birth. Nancy began delivering later than we had predicted. The calf was big; in fact, it was too big for her to deliver alone. Their hips locked. Dad had the chain and tackles looped around the calf's ankles—standard procedure in births we assisted—when he realized that the calf needed to be pulled immediately. He gave a hell of a pull and fell flat on the wet concrete. I knelt over the calf to see if it was breathing. She was. Dad was fine, once he got off the barn floor, and happy that it was a heifer. A couple of months later he had to visit the doctor, though, to get the elbow he landed on lanced. I thought that calf, Dora, was worth every bit of Dad's pain.

Dora was one of the first sold when the cows went to auction. The auction went in a predictable way—the pretty good animals first to raise interest and bidding, and the best animals toward the middle. As I understand it, the sale went well, partly because some of the animals, such as Dora and her calf, went as "the girls' 4-H animals, blue ribbon winners." We averaged $800 a cow.

Although we farmed in old barns and did not borrow money to expand or remodel, we were consistently recognized for the purity and quality of our milk. This was a sore spot with the milk inspector, the man who certified the farm as sanitary. He really just wanted us to build new barns, so he'd come once a year and make us do lots of repair work and surface changes and then grudgingly pass us for inspection. Despite the old barns, our somatic cell count was among the lowest in the county; in my scrapbook I have recently discovered two certificates for high-quality milk production for the last two years we farmed—1985 and 1986. We must have received the last certificate months after the milking cows left the farm.

We were lucky. We chose to sell out. The sale wasn't held on our farm, amid our barns; I didn't see the animals auctioned. We weren't forced out by creditors; we didn't have to sell the land. Most importantly, we did not participate in the Whole Herd Buy-Out Program, the government program where, if your bid was accepted, all of your cows were bought and then slaughtered for beef in an attempt to eliminate the milk surplus. We did not have to sacrifice the years that we had spent poring over breeding tables and bull catalogues. We controlled the sale of the cows, so that we sold out ethically, as we had farmed.

■ ■ ■

What it meant to be a girl growing up on a small farm is tangled, paradoxical. When times got really bad, when we could no longer afford the hired hand and we needed to help with chores, nothing else was dropped in terms of our responsibilities and commitments. We still took the hardest courses in school, ran track, played basketball, participated in school plays, and got ready for college. Then, after hours at school, we would come home, eat something, and help with chores. One of us would go down to help during the milking, sweeping hay into the stalls, scraping shit. Another one of us would go down later, when the milking was almost done, to help finish up. We'd get back to the house from the late shift at about nine. I started waking up at four-thirty or five in the morning to study the chemistry I hadn't finished the night before. Despite the stresses of the work, I was fascinated by the process of farming and constantly asked questions about the way things worked.

What we didn't do was work with machinery. We didn't drive tractors or repair engines. In some respects, the reason we didn't operate farm machinery is the same as the reason that we didn't have a bull on the farm until we were old enough to understand the danger present in two thousand pounds of angry animal. Working with the machinery was a good way to lose a limb or get killed. However, since we were not exposed to the mechanical aspects of things, we missed a crucial aspect of training to be a farmer. Small farming requires generalists, people who are able to do a variety of things in a variety of ways, as conditions require. Not knowing how to weld, change the oil in a tractor, or even drive the tractor would be a handicap if any of us attempted to farm on our own. Traditionally, one's husband would be the source of mechanical knowledge. In reality, since the three of us were all girls, we were exposed to much less outright sexism than our female friends. Their brothers drove tractors, plowed fields, and raked hay while the girls stood in the haymow in the ninety-degree summer heat and stacked fifty-pound square-bales.

When I was twelve or so, Dad did try to teach me to drive a tractor. He was considering buying a twenty-thousand-dollar Ford tractor, a 7700 that has rear tires taller than I am. We had it on the farm for a test drive period, and one day after school, Dad put me on it. I was holding down both the clutch and the brake, and he was standing between the rear wheels and the front wheels when I popped the clutch. The tractor lurched forward toward one of the smaller buildings. Dad leapt on the tractor on top of me and out of the reach of the wheel. He stopped the tractor, but that was the end of tractor driving for me. When I learned to drive a car at sixteen, a friend of the family taught me; Dad still hates it when I drive him anywhere. For a while after I almost killed my father with the tractor, I imagined that soon he would teach me to drive one of the smaller tractors, so I could rake hay with him during the summer. I imagined the feeling of driving around the fields on a tractor, making something.

■ ■ ■

I have no tidy way to end this piece. What surprises me is how painful it is, even after almost a decade, to think about what's gone. After all the education I've had, I have no theory in which to place these experiences. While I profess liberalism, what I really think is in its way deeply conservative—that if more people farmed, the United States would be a better place. My values are intimately linked with the land, with saving and preserving, with ideas of home and place shaping a life. In the end, what I believe in is long-term, collective ownership of land, in stewardship and care by communities with ties to specific pieces of ground, and in the ideals of domestic permanence created by memory and tradition.

What I see happening in the decade since my family has stopped farming is almost apocalyptic. The idea that a growth hormone won't change cows or their milk doesn't make sense to me. The idea that a thousand-animal herd can be accurately monitored for disease and infection is completely unrealistic, not to mention that a thousand head of dairy cattle will act as a source of pollution. Farmers are not making the decision that bigger is better, and this decision does not involve the consumer, either, except indirectly—the American consumer has always demanded cheap food.

In the end, I'm happy that we still own our farmland, because regardless of what happens to the food supply at large, there is still a possibility for me to return, in some way, to a kind of moral agriculture based on nurturing, care, commitment, and conservation of the land for the next generation. For my daughters, at least, the idea of a small farm is still a possibility.

On the Bridge

Late Sunday afternoon, driving east through Pennsylvania.
A hush behind the Last Exit Before Toll signs.
Love is asleep in the passenger seat and may never

wake up again. One at a time, you unclench
your hands from the wheel; shaking them out,
you think for the first time of work, the office,

life flooding back like blood to a numb limb.
You think: those predawn mornings, too blue-black
for your dull head, Love left lying in the bed,

that ugly hour too quick for coffee. You think:
the whir of the computer and its white screen, bits
of you in its heart and brain and teeth.

There's a rush, a commotion, or else
it is only you there typing, alphabetizing, playing
mother to plastic, metal, and paper. Either way,

nothing more is asked of you than blankness. Later,
it is all you ask of yourself, sipping wine, cooking
dinner, bringing two plates to the television.

Here in the cold car you blink,
you reassume your life, no less tired than it was
on Friday. Love stirs and leans toward the window.

You get the toll ready, three cool quarters in your palm.
You are on the bridge, its long and right design,
the cars spaced with perfect symmetry, one by one by one.

The Sun Goes Down in the Suburbs

Seems to me my days have just been split up and spent,
wrangling in my head, drifting in and out.

Yet I usually find myself in the same place. At the kitchen
counter, sitting in front of a bowl of dried-up soup and a cup of
cold tea, the only one here.

I snap off the TV before the news comes on, look out the
window above the sink. I watch the sun go down in the suburbs,
orange reflections on the windows of the house across the street.

My boredom dissolves when all the noise stops and the
movement quits and the people go away. I sink down and dirty
into my element. Read an old book again, make a can of soup,
play some solitaire.

I feel the possible in me, stacking and folding, reams of
quiet paper.

The Trip from HECK: Day Two, Wednesday, 8/16

Leaving Christianburg, Virginia, tired and too early. It's slightly less muggy than yesterday—you can't see the air. The sky is still the blue of an ancient pair of stone-washed jeans made pale and soft by rinse cycles and tumble drys. Dad got a ticket for speeding, so we're now on cruise control at 65 mph.

I've been writing to Josh. Josh is this really cool guy I met at CTY (nerd camp) this summer. He looks a little like Lurch from the Addams family, only with shoulder-length, dirty-blond hair he wears in French braids. And energy. He's hyperactive—literally, he's on medication for it—except for Friday night dances when he skips the pills and dons dresses, makeup, and certain satin underwire garments belonging to me. He then takes the name of Betty and/ or Candi and dances with a herd of his friends, oddly enough, all female. I really like him, in many ways. He is just so...everything. Perfect. Josh is a god. If only he'd shave....

Only one stumbling block to my adoration, and her name is Kim. The love of Josh's life. Sigh. She's really nice, though—funny and intelligent. I'm happy they have each other. Besides, lovers desert. True friends remain, whether you want them to or not. Trust me, I know.

The mountains are shaped like bread crumbs here: lumpy, craggy, steep, yet small. They look like chunks of larger mountains that were shaken off in a winter shiver. Some are little and humpy, some perfectly rounded as if something shaped them to the contours of a hand, as if the land was meant to be caressed. Kudzu has covered the land, the way clothing hides the curves of a body. The earth is red-orange. I have never seen red dirt before. In the north, the earth is dark brown—chocolate, almost. Here, the ground is like the bricks of an old, old building, crumbling redly away to the touch of wind or hand.

In Tennessee now. We stopped at the Welcome Center. We always do. I went into the bathroom, put water on my face, washed my hands, adjusted my hat, and began putting on lip gloss. A little girl with curly blonde hair was watching me with big eyes. She was clutching a paper towel. She took her mother's hand and started to walk out, still carrying the towel. Her mother noticed and threw it away. "She was so busy watching you put your lipstick on that she forgot," the mother, also blonde and probably in her early thirties, said. I made an affirmative noise. I make lots of affirmative noises.

We stopped at a Wendy's for lunch. The ground is strawberry-blond now. Still lots of climbing vines clothing the trees and ground. Mother Nature should have been a fashion designer.

There was this green river a few minutes after the Wendy's. Not a bad green—a rather nice green, even if it did resemble toxic waste.

Dollywood. We are passing freaking *Dollywood*. Only in Tennessee. You couldn't have Dollywood in Philadelphia. You couldn't. I mean, maybe you could have Boyz II Menwood. Green Daywood. Nine Inch Nailswood. Huh huh. I'd go there. Closer: The Ride. Yes, I'd *definitely* go there.

The earth is redder here. It varies between red-gold and red-brown, the exact color of Nana Visitor's hair. Nana is my favorite actress; she's on "Star Trek: Deep Space Nine." She plays Kira, the bitchy one with the cool nose. Watch the show; it's cool 'n stuff.

We're driving through Knoxville. I can see the huge gold ball on top of the building from the World's Fair. No traffic for the first part. We pass the city in just a few minutes. A tape with Rod Stewart's "Maggie May" is playing. The first time I ever heard this song was when Melissa Etheridge played it on her MTV Unplugged. "Wake up Maggie, I think I got something to say to you."

Melissawood. Hmm. It's an idea.

Heavy traffic a few minutes outside of the city. A hubcap on the side of the road. An ambulance siren. I pull the pillowcase back over my window to block the hot southern sun. Very hot. We turn off the air conditioning and open the windows. The air is the same temperature I like my tea. I'm an herbal tea freak. I even have a water bottle holding a tea bag with me on the trip. The air is so hot that it burns my ears after only a moment's contact. I hate sun and sunburns. My skin is fair; I burn in about twenty minutes.

I miss my computer. I have a really lovely Macintosh Quadra 700. Big and huge and large. I call it Big Mac. We also have a (practically antique) Commodore 64c named Goldie, a CD player, two tape decks, an amplifier, and my clock radio. All at home.

Are you getting sick of me talking about the dirt? Well, sorry, but it's about all I can see. Dirt and trees and hills and roads and my brother. Besides, it is a very noticeable difference (Random remembrance...*Just noticeable difference (jnd): the difference in frequency there must be for a person to detect the difference in frequency fifty percent of the time.*—from *Psychology* by David Myers, taught in "Introduction to Psychology," CTY, Hamilton campus, second session, teacher Pat Phillips, Ph.D., TA Tonya). Trees look the same in Pennsylvania. Hills look the same in Pennsylvania. Roads look the same in Pennsylvania. My brother looks the same in Pennsylvania. But the dirt doesn't look the same in Pennsylvania. It looks...different.

My counselor at camp, Stacy, had the best food. Wurms 'n Durt. Gummy worms in crushed Oreo cookies. She brought them out on the last day. "Anybody want some dirty worms?" Very happy, Stacy made us.

We're passing some big granite mountains that look suspiciously like the Adirondacks. Driving on the side of a huge mountain, staring into a huge hazy valley that seems to go on forever, is exhilarating. The rocks are intensely different.

Central time. 3:22 p.m. central time. So now Joan's only three time zones away....

Joan is a girl I met at camp. Tall, slightly overweight, rather pretty, with a propensity for wearing long skirts. She's from Fairbanks, Alaska. Josh, I miss her. I mean, you get a friend, a soulmate, a fellow writer, another member of the Cult of Josh, and then she goes away. Far away. As in, other side of the country away.

She remains here in my soul, at least. She truly loves Josh. I mean, *real* love, not what passes for it in high school. She wrote down her feelings for him once in the form of this rambling internal monologue, and then she let me read it. It was pure, untempered by the basic lusts that run through the teenage body and ravage it so. She really loved him, God bless her. Her words made me realize that she could never be forgotten, that in my every thought about Josh there should also be a cross-reference to Joan, that I can never forget her. I mean, if I try, how hard can it be to remember someone like her? My favorite image of her immortalizes her to me—a bisexual writer with a heart of gold wearing a black shirt and a "hot pink skirt so bright it makes you look for the off switch" (Josh's words) singing "Bye, bye Miss American Pie" in a lovely alto and holding up two fingers in a silent salute to her love while salt tears carry mascara to her chin. That picture is forever painted on the screen saver of my mind. She will always remain there.

We just saw a beautiful vista—mountains on all sides, a huge cut-away rock face on the right. Breathtaking.

Half an hour at a rest stop, with cold soda for everyone. I practiced dribbling a soccer ball, kicking it around. I'm not a bad player; my school has a coed team. Hmm. I refilled the water bottle that Joan gave me on the last day of camp and put the used tea bag back in it. It hasn't bled yet.

Dear Josh, we are south now, aren't we? Even the sky is bleached white by the sun. Everything changes down here. It's odd that none of my preconceptions of "Southern USA" are being challenged. Maybe it's because I was right. Maybe it's because all highways look the same.

I find one major problem with being in the south—too many country music stations. I mean, just one punk/alternative station. The Offspring or Weezer or even Green Day for Josh's sake.

Nashville. Opryland. "Music City." It's right here in front of me. Somewhere. I cannot see a single building or billboard to distinguish this from everything else. Oh, an ad for a Hard Rock Cafe. That's something.

Ah, here we go. City. A little like Philly. Big. A city, not a burg. Yay!!!

Well, bye bye, Nashville. Next stop: Memphis, Tennessee. On the anniversary of Elvis' death. Josh help us, or Elvis help us, or maybe Gene Roddenberry help us. As long as somebody does.

Shh. Be wwery wwery qwiet. We're hunting Taco Bells. I've tried to explain my theory that there *are* no Taco Bells in Tennessee. We are still searching. What is so bad about a Burger King or Wendy's or, if need be, even a Waffle House (whatever they are; they're a southern phenomenon). I mean, damn, I might even lower myself to a McDonald's—but only if the need truly arises.

Supplies are dwindling. We'll have to make a supply run in Memphis, or maybe we'll just go without. Choice A is preferable.

We just got out of a huge traffic jam. The sun is low, and red like a radioactive cherry. Maybe more like the construction road signs. Yes, just that orangey-red color.

Dinner @ Arby's. Finally.

Car trouble. I hope we get a move on. It's 8:01 p.m. central and we need to get two hours down the road. Oh, fuck this trip!

Just got word—no open garages this time of night. We're getting a room at a local Econolodge and screwing Memphis. The alternator belt's loose. We'll go to an Amoco in the morning. Of course, this means we're going all the way to Plano tomorrow if we get the car fixed. *If.*

Excerpted from the unpublished book-length manuscript Debbie's House: The Trip from HECK! *by Emily Regan Wills.*

UNTITLED (SUNFLOWER)   8" x 10"   **R. TERI MEMOLO**
photo collage contact print

My photographs are very much like my poetry. Everything is like a great collage to me. When I combine things, I find that I am somewhere in there. It is more than an aperture shutting. I have constructed these images from bottom to top. I like the idea of putting things where they don't belong.

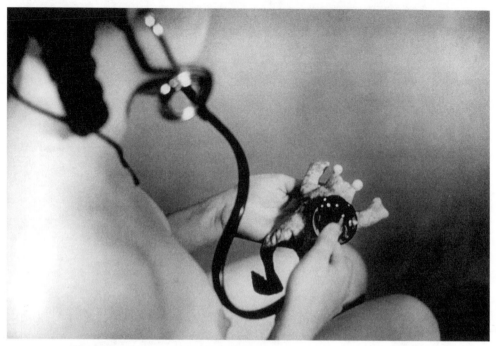

UNTITLED (FROG)   11" x 16"   **R. TERI MEMOLO**
monochromatic color coupler print

My models were so subtle; they possessed the restraint to carry the idea without letting their egos penetrate the photographs.

Avocado Security

It's strange that in Los Angeles they call this air, yet here I am breathing it, being it, and occasionally wondering how I got here. When it's 4:00 a.m., like now, the 24-hour donut shops (and there are a lot of them) seem both haunting and comforting. It's as if my body—in the window, munching on a glazed-raised—could be the soft and brutal essence of an Edward Hopper painting.

Right. I'm going home after hanging out in Hollywood. I have lots of time to think while the engine guns seventy-five down the highway. There's no one out here, not even cops. My brain goes into a Narnian swirl.

Can you feel anything at all, except when you're falling from a great height or getting the shit beat out of you? You live vicariously through boxes of icons or strive for some hellishly daredevilish experience like hang gliding, because that means you will have really lived, right? My generation screams for prime time and bungee jumping; well, some of us, anyway. All my life I have been pummelled with information, pulled into vast quantities of attention-grabbing, ever-spinning images that tell me how to live, who I'm allowed to be, and what the proper behavior patterns are for living an acceptable life. This monolith of images from television, radio, movies, newspapers, billboards, and so on has been trying to get our attention for countless seasons; its messages keep working to "one up" everything we've seen before. This century is amazing, you can change channels from "Blood Fist" to "Mary Tyler Moore" in less than a second, and your brain is okay with that. I mean, it's more than channel surfing, it's that, well, we *are* the Jetsons, and it's crept up on me, I'm not ready for this, I feel obsolete. I'm only twenty-three and wondering if anything I'm living is real.

I catch the corner of my eye in the rearview mirror. Like I said, I've got a lot of time to think in this car. I'm a goddamn Gen-X lesbian. Hollywood is all about lesbians right now; there are at least five lesbian-themed movies in production as we speak, it's all the rage to be a lesbo, a "Lipstick Lesbian" from what is said in medialand. Ha! What's funny to me is who this town thinks lesbians are. I know that all of us don't have shoulder pads, ice picks, perfectly coifed hair, and flawless makeup. I'm so far away from that...except maybe the ice pick. But you wouldn't know from all the smarmy ads they've got on queer magazines and flyers. The monolith needs more money for its ads, and it needs fresh material, and new interest groups from which to take blood. "What's the public never seen before? Lesbians! Gays! Bisexuals! Let's get 'em and woo their fantasies to the likes of Absolut Vodka and AT&T!" We used to be taboo, unacceptable pariahs and freaks fit for beating—now we're cool. In Hollywood, you can flake on people, fuck them over, take their money, steal their ideas and their clothes. There's only one rule: Do it with a smile! Those ad agency nimrods wouldn't know a dyke from a can of almonds, but they're trying really hard, brushing their teeth and everything.

But you know, if they don't get me now, it's no great loss, because they got me long ago when my eyes were new. TV is life, it's fuel for growth and be-coming part of the social circuit. Y'know, I just loved Jo on "Facts of Life." I wanted to be big and tough and have a motorcycle just like hers; a dyke seedling's research could be found in her behavior, surely. She was different from all the rest, and even as a young tyke, I could tell the networks were getting paranoid, because they gave her a boyfriend and started putting her in dresses, and then they layered her hair. Already I was sensing the thing TV was doing: "See? She's not a lez, she was just a tomboy, and with the right schooling, your masculine, self-assertive daughter can also grow up to become a productive member of society!" Oh, but we're all brothers and sisters un-der the big, glowing screen.

Maybe in 2095, we'll have growing dynasties who hail Jif peanut butter as their crest, and they'll have an ongoing feud with the Skippy family. It'll be a caste system, where the generic brand users are the untouchables. And all families will live in fear under the fascist regime of Nike, which is fighting the axis of Adidas, Reebok, and Converse for more world power. Maybe I'm get-ting a little out there with this, but does it seem completely implausible?

I suppose the beauty of a brand-name system hierarchy is that, even if you only have five cents, you can still buy something, and that makes you part of the warm fuzzy system of consumer breakdown. Maybe if you buy all organic food, you will be reincarnated as a cybernetic amoeba in a vitamin pill.

Have I been driving for fifteen minutes, or fifty? I've left the radio on static and the car's almost out of gas.

I sort of like the "ringed eye" feeling, when I haven't had sleep and all the gas station lollipop signs have an especially endearing quality about them. I ease down the off-ramp, past the Wonderbread outlet, and into the yellow Shell Station. I drive a '68 Mustang, red with dots and patches of primer and very dusty. I feel like I've just come out of a time warp, and my spaceship is covered with interplanetary cactus residue. I'm wearing a security jacket—it's not my job, it was a gift from a friend—kind of raggedy, but convincing enough, I guess. Generally, it makes people leave me alone, like they're paranoid I'm going to arrest them or something. The lights make me squint for a second. I skim the cement and open the door to the bulletproof snack room. A man is behind the counter; he looks like he's from India, bald, very tan, about forty-five. He wants to know my story. We go through a soft shuffle.

"What security company do you work for?" I glance at the avocado pin on my sleeve; someone put it there when I was in Austin.

"Uh, Avocado Security," I mumble. He's never heard of them. I haven't the time to get into full, interactive-person mode, and I'm amazed I can comprehend sentences this late at night.

"Pays well?" He cocks his head to one side.

"Yuh." I hold six dollars in space, the fluorescence accentuating aisles of candy wrappers.

"Are you married?" He's not being a putz or anything.

I say, "No." He looks at me like he can't believe it and he has to lean in for a closer look.

"How old are you?"

As annoyed as I am, I'm compelled to tell him. "I'm twenty-three."

"Ah, you are young," he says. "It's when the baby wonders where you are, and the husband letting you work...that's a problem. But, no husband, no baby, no problem!" He's grinning.

I'm perplexed, and the Slushie machine is churning a hypnotic melody...8oz...12oz...16oz.... How long will this interaction go on?

"Why aren't you married?"

So I ease my six bucks towards him and explain cheerily, "Well, I love women."

And he takes my money, says "Oh!" laughing a great booming laugh. It's not mocking laughter or confused laughter, but kind of like he's solved a riddle. He's the legacy of his ancestors, far bigger than a Shell station. The sound of his smile stays with me through the parking lot. After I'm done filling the tank, I get in the car and survey the dashboard. I back out of the driveway, take a last look at the station, and the guy gives me a wave; I wave back and head onto the interstate. You know, that whole situation had the potential to be much weirder than it was; it could have been unpleasant, it could've been an angry match of shouting, it could've been a night of lies, like I could've told him I was married and it was my husband's jacket. Those answers and situations will float in space forever in infinite combinations.

I'm by myself again, unscathed, amused, far from the Shell station, far from everything, in fact. I'm back with my thoughts. This will go on for some time, because I have a ways to go before I'm home.

I have no idea what that guy back at the gas station was into, but his laugh was good thunder, and it rarely rains here in the desert. The sun isn't up, I'm flying down the highway, and truth be known, in spite of it all, with this dumbshit air, 4:00 a.m. in LA can be kind of all right.

DREAM OF A QUEERBIT FIEND   JULIANNA PARR

I draw to satiate myself, to contemplate and enjoy—it is what I know. I wish to fish for issues, or none at all, and portray trappings of SURREAL, BIZARRE plains of existence in dyke/gender/hell/loss/modern life etc. senses. "I don't really know if I'm here" is basically the theme of everything I do.

DREAM of a QUEERBIT FIEND

TV Child

tv child
what was it like
before direct dial?
spinning 45s
on the stereo console
watching cable
kimba the white lion
and speed racer
global village vietnam
nightly news saigon
dim sum view of what's going on
who was the sla anyway?
everyone was so uptight
willing to fight
for some real or imagined cause
donald le gre died at the scene
in a shootout with the lapd
sara jane parker
squeeky la fromme
pulled out their guns
taking pot shots at the president
they got sent through the
california penal system

like charlie and sirhan sirhan
shootout in the courtroom
with angela davis
alcatraz gets taken over
by native americans
harvey milk and george moscone
get shot by a homophobic malcontent
and the sentiment sends
police cars on fire
while the zodiac killer runs loose
in blue spruce park
down the street
from my grandmother's house

Stopped at the Tracks

the Chevy falters, then stalls;
you swear softly, a train
slows into the city.
Like an opossum, the boy sleeps between us
on the dusty seat,
oblivious to the key's dead turns,
the muttering engine, clanging red lights, and your
voice
which now breaks with rage;
the hood's green paint is buckled,
peeling.
As the rails rush black before me
I hear the long scream
of the whistle, thunder,
your foul mouth filling my ears enough
to overpower
the grate of steel.

Soldier-like, rust-colored box cars roll,
Southern Pacific,
hesitant in their procession,
"Fuck! Goddamn fucking truck!"

                        I watch your knuckles whiten
                        as you grip the steering wheel:
I want to laugh.
                        This truck won't cower
                        wishing to be dirt;
it won't respond to your flat palm strikes,
your drunken frenzies,
                        but I know your fury
                        will soon fall on me
and I'll feel
            the bite of your hands.
My back's already blistered
                        with cigarette burns,
scarred worse than these
                        green paint welts,
                        and my ribs cracked twice.

Some freight doors stand open,
                        the spaces dark, barren,
and the boy sleeps.
                        Five years since he was born,
and you first broke
                        my ribs; your anger comes
all the time now,
                        and my belly is big again,
big and ripe
            like the moon.

Mulberry Tree

My uncle Leland looked like my father—the same lean six-foot-four body, except Deddy had big, bulging muscles and was getting a beer belly, and Leland was thin and muscular like a runner.

I remember Leland with a bloody face, blood that stained and dyed brown the cement steps of our front porch, like the crushed-mulberry stains on the cement steps in the alley. Deddy had stabbed Leland—"in self-defense," Mama said over and over on the phone.

The kids didn't go to the funeral. When the adults returned to our house for food, I felt guilty. I couldn't believe that they came back to our house. Deddy had killed their father, uncle, brother, son. Leland was dead and his frozen blood was stepped on by funeral shoes entering the killer's house. Maybe they thought the stain was mulberry.

■ ■ ■

The stain was there months later, after the cold cement steps had thawed and dried from the heat.

That summer I turned nine and the house two doors down burned up, leaving a vacant lot, a set of three cement steps that led from the alley to the missing house, and a mulberry tree that must have been growing in that back-yard for years. As many times as I had gone down the alley, I had never seen that tree before.

As the summer droned on, I forgot what the lot had ever looked like with a house. On weekends the lot became our baseball field, run-across field, football field, and milkweed-fight field. The lot: a mulberry tree, a field of buried broken glass, and three cement steps that we used as a recovery box whenever someone would get the wind knocked out of 'em.

In July Mama and Deddy reopened Leland's tavern and his neighborhood grocery and renamed them Blackburn's Bar & Grill and Blackburn's Market. Mama ran the store on one corner of Delmar and St. Louis Avenue, and Deddy ran the tavern across the street. That summer we went from being a family of ten who travelled in an old Country Squire station wagon—with a constantly falling-off muffler and parts frequently removed by Deddy when he was drunk and not wanting Mama to escape his punches—to a family of ten who owned a new black Cadillac and a white van with a desert landscape on the side.

For the rest of the summer Mama and Deddy kinda disappeared and I had to stay home with Benson, Daryl, and Jessie while Towanda and Lamont went to marching-band camp and LaVern and Roscoe worked in the store. Every morning I made breakfast for three, dressed them, and put them in the back-yard, Daryl and Jessie in the playpen so they wouldn't fall into the basement hole. I'd go to the basement, put a load of clothes in the washing machine, bring up the load that was taken off the line the night before, and iron in Mama's room while I watched "Felix the Cat," "Happy Days," and "The Young & the Restless." Then I'd make two sandwiches with two cookies on the side and a bowl of ABC soup for Jessie. I'd change Daryl and Jessie's diapers and give them all a nap on the floor in Mama's room where the air conditioner kept it cool.

When I was sure they had fallen asleep and the one-hundred-degree sun was just about to reach the clothesline, I'd go out to the laundry pole, with its dia-mond-shaped web of rope and steel, and hang clothes. Then I'd go in and make my own lunch—garlic baloney with lettuce (if we had any) and mustard on bread, and two sandwich cream cookies. I'd sit in the kitchen, checking past the door of Mama's room to see if the little bodies had sat up on their pallets.

My loneliness was like the loneliness I felt when I was four. The big kids were at school and Mama was always tired with Benson growing in her belly. She napped almost all day, leaving me waiting for the mailman's footsteps on the porch and, later, the sound of the school bell.

■ ■ ■

I knew I would feel less lonely if I took down the clothes and washed and hung another load, but instead I always sat at the kitchen table, which I'd cleaned with a dishrag that smelled like Palmolive, eggs, and bacon grease. Through the back door I could hear kids playing in the shade or in the water at the fire hydrant. Two doors down I could hear Angela and Denise yelling at their little brother and sister, who were also pinned in the house till their mother got home from work. At least I could go out back to hang clothes. Their voices made me long for 5:30 when Mama closed the store and the world came back to keep me company.

Before long, Daryl, who was always cross, would start crying, or Jessie would start blowing spit bubbles, or Benson would start lifting and banging his leg, and the worst part of the day was over. I could put them out to play on the back porch, where the only shade hovered long enough for me to put up the child gate and the play pen and watch my story while Pledging and Windexing. The closing music to "The Guiding Light" made me feel empty, like air was filling my belly. I had an hour and a half to finish cleaning, take the dinner meat out of the freezer, and put the clothes away before Mama got home. I timed myself by seeing how much I could do in the time my wooden Fisher Price clock could play its tick-tock song. I'd wind it over and over as I went from room to room.

■ ■ ■

Mama only let me go to the store one day that summer—she made Lavern stay home. Mama had always said I was better off watch'n the boys than get'n in the way. "You too young to really help by ring'n up things on the cash register. Besides, I don't want you down there eat'n up all the profit." So when I did go, I sat on a stool behind the counter and ate up all the profit.

That day I ate as much as I could in Leland's old store. Whenever Mama went to the meat counter to slice baloney or Braunschweiger and Roscoe was sweeping, I snatched a bag of Fritos off the clip and a Hostess cupcake off the shelf. I took a handful of corn chips and a big bite of cupcake, just getting the salt and chocolate mashed up enough to swallow. The back of my throat was getting scratched by the chips, but I hurried and filled my mouth again. I did the whole snack in three mouthfuls, and I had five snacks that morning.

At lunchtime Mama had Deddy cross the street from the tavern to watch the store while she ran me home. I insisted that I was still hungry and took home a baloney sandwich. For some reason she didn't hit me or yell, just kept eyes on the road and said, "I cain't have you eat'n all the profit."

■ ■ ■

The only time Mama hit me that summer was the Saturday I came running in from playing on the lot with a fireball jawbreaker stuck in my throat. She set the pressing comb back on the eye, punched me in the back, and kept pressing Towanda's hair. I went back to the lot and hid in the mulberry tree, waiting for Angela or Denise or somebody to come back out and play. The branches were thick and low, the trunk was thick and sturdy, and the layers of branches went high enough for me to see backyards and the tops of garages. I saw Mama come out on the back porch and yell for me, and I ignored her. I knew she couldn't see my brown face and legs mixed up in those dark green leaves, brown-grey limbs, and black-purple berries. I wasn't going to go in so she could make me feed the baby or sweep up the hair, saying, "When ya see someth'n that needs done around here—do it." And then she'd get ready to leave for Saturday night at the tavern, and I'd be stuck.

When no one came back to the lot to play, I ate mulberries, and when I felt like puking mulberries, I threw some, trying to hit the top step of the three cement steps. When I had made a stain as big as the one on our front porch, I climbed down and wiped off the seeds and put on a little dirt, then brushed it off to make the stain look dry. I tried walking up the steps without noticing the stain. I smiled and walked and talked like I was greeting someone at their front door. Every time I stepped on the stain, I heard Leland's head hitting, cracking on the top step, and felt the rubber skin of my Betsy Wetsy doll puncture under the pressure of my fingernails. Still no one came out to play. So I played until Leland fell through the glass of the front door, pieces of broken glass falling, muted. I played until Leland got up to run and no sounds were carried by the bottoms of his shoes, his hands and knees grinding in glass on cement. I played until Deddy's knife connected under Leland's chin, and Leland fell back. His head did not hit and make a cracking noise like Christmas nuts in Mama's palms, but hit the top step and bounced off, the knife spinning in blood.

■ ■ ■

Black, polished shoes had stepped on the stain, over and over, and come into the house to cry with Mama and Deddy, and I felt so guilty. All the people my father called family, but who we rarely saw, were in our house. Some of them lived right here in St. Louis, some even in our neighborhood, but we never saw them either. These people were at our house after the funeral and Deddy only went to jail for one day, so he was at the house, too.

Leland's oldest daughter was bending over a kitchen drawer, asking me where the knives were. Her skirt was black lace with a hem that came only to her butt, and she was wearing black fishnet hose and no underwear.

The sound of stainless steel came back, unmuted—my cousin finding a good knife and sharpening it on Mama's stone, the knife hitting cold cement, which turned red then brown. She stared at me. My eyes were fixed on her hand and the knife, and I wondered how her velour black heels could have stepped over the brown stain.

FROM MOTHER TO SON 15" X 20" **SABRINA DAVIS**
watercolor & charcoal on paper

I create images that have left indelible imprints in my head. The spiritual connections between the Earth and all beings are more easily captured by eclectic media forms: paint, tile, found objects, wire, and truth. If the spirit of the piece passes through the viewer and to the universe, I've done something.

one minute filled

see this picture of my parents
my mother's one foot curved inward
like a child who needs a friend
and father's collar unbuttoned
leaving him open for criticism

see them sit
between columns
of the Grand Hotel
the wind is captured
in their hair

the sound of the paper
as it falls back into
the box

Afterward

Sometimes I blame you. Most often the blaming starts at night, when you are sleeping and I lie awake, caught inside your breathing. As your body slopes against mine in the dark, your hand feels skinny and childish clutching my breasts. Your lips feel flaccid against my neck, and I feel trapped in your sleep-embrace.

■ ■ ■

Once I begin blaming you, it becomes easier and easier. You send me a suggestive kiss while I lie in the bathtub, unhappy in the cooling water—how could you look at me that way? You forget to feed the cats, who then worm under my feet, insistent and angry. You leave the ashtray next to the bed where I can't help but knock it over in a silver-grey shower. *How could you,* I keep asking silently, bitter when you eat the leftover curry or finish the tampons without buying a new box. *How could you let something like that happen to me?*

Of course I know it wasn't your fault. I'm not stupid. I know who to blame: him. Sure, that's easy. I could blame him if his face showed up in my dreams or if I thought about him late at night. But I don't. It's easier to think about you, because you were there then. You're still here.

■ ■ ■

Actually you and I had fought that night. Remember? I don't know about what. Maybe the chick with the shaved head you had flirted with at the party the weekend before.

We were enclosed in a booth at one of the dense, smoky pubs you liked to take me to, and you had ordered black and tans for both of us. We could barely hear each other because of the football game roaring from TV sets on either end of the bar. All around us, red-faced men would suddenly jam themselves into the air when something happened in the game, yowl at one another before they'd subside, and you'd glance away from our conversation to the TV for a moment, not quite long enough for me to complain. It was the kind of place I never would have walked into without you. I never would have looked twice at the green and yellow storefront with the neon shamrocks and lit-up pit bull in the window, but I've been back since, when it wasn't football season. I liked the varnished, oily look of the tables and the beer-on-tap and the way nobody said anything to us at all.

You stared into your half-pint and licked at the corners of your mouth while I talked, and I remember the angry buzz of my own voice, but not my words. I remember your face: freckled, blunt, and a little confused. What seems sad to me now is how angry your confusion made me. You'd apologize and I'd fling myself back in my seat. *What for?* I'd ask you.

You'd turn away, shrug so that the chains on your leather jacket would wring against each other. *I don't know,* you kept saying.

Then I don't want your apology, I'd say, with extra, angry spit in my mouth, consciously twisting my eyes away from your ruddy face. I told you, *Don't say it if you don't know what you're sorry for.*

We left the bar, pushing through the excited crowd of men who never met our eyes. Outside, the stars were slung low and the streets were slushy. Tears scraped their way out of my eyes, slow and leaky. Before the fight, before we'd gone into the pub, we had been shoving each other playfully, slamming up against each other's bodies. You had lifted me up onto your shoulders while I wriggled, screaming, and passersby had watched us, stunned. But after the fight, we walked in silence. Disoriented by the tears I was trying to blink back, I skidded on some ice. You held my arm but I jerked myself away, so you walked ahead of me, indifferent.

■ ■ ■

I blame you for it because nothing like that ever happened to me when I was alone. Men tried to pick me up or asked me annoying questions—but nothing like that. Together, duplicated, twinned, in our leather jackets and spiky hair, it happened to us all the time. One early summer evening, we stood downtown, me kissing you earnestly on your forehead and you pressing against my kisses in that mute, endearing way you had. You were holding onto my waist. We had only been dating a few months, so we considered running into each other that night one of those marvelous surprises that meant we were destined to be together.

The man who screamed at us wore a Red Sox cap and jeans; he was white with a fleshy, mottled face. He yelled something about perverts and killing us and hell. Here's where it gets blurry for me, because I don't remember him. I remember us. I remember you. I remember how he moved closer to me with a threatening fist and how I moved closer to him, unafraid, sure I couldn't be hurt with a crowd of people watching. I remember taunting him, *You're just jealous, 'cause for sure no woman would look twice at you,* and I remember my satisfaction at watching his face double up with rage and his skin shiver and his offer to shut my mouth for good.

You stepped between us and you were quiet, talking to him in a language I didn't entirely understand, the language of someone who had grown up pretty close to where he had grown up. You leaned against the slight air between him and us—you were angular and threatening and I watched your strong back, your ironed white T-shirt, feeling proud and safe. He stepped away from you, sweating, and loud still. People behind us applauded and I swung around to see a semicircle of young men and women in the shimmer of lights from a record store. One gave us the thumbs-up sign.

Babe, I told you, *let's get out of here.*

■ ■ ■

Another time we were walking back from a Fred & Ginger movie fest, in slender rain, holding hands. From time to time you swung me around and I tried to be graceful for you, even in combat boots. When three frat boys passed us, splashing mud from puddles, I ignored them, but you slammed your feet against the pavement and turned around. From the expression on your face I knew something was wrong. I pulled my skirt down lower and tried to look mean, ready to back you up.

You pinched me on the butt, you told one man. Your blonde hair was flattened by the rain and your face looked soft, angelic. The rain curled down your cheek companionably.

Oh please, he said. He had stopped with his friends. His shiny green jacket was halfway zipped and he wore chunky rings. *I did not touch your dyke butt,* he said.

You shook your head and moved closer to him, looking fearless. *You pinched me on the ass and I'm going to kick your ass,* you said to him. All three looked at us and pulled their young faces into sneers. One jutted out his lower lip and shoved me on the shoulder, and my body jolted back, but I refused to fall. I began hitting at him—ineffectual slaps on his arm. But you, you sent the boy with the rings sprawling onto the pavement, his face scraped against the sludgy ground. He staggered up and they ran away, leaping over puddles, while we watched and jeered. When they were out of sight, you wrapped your arm around my shoulders, calm and triumphant.

■ ■ ■

And there were other times, I could go into them all: the time you took the pamphlets out of a young skinhead's hands on the train, tore them up and then blocked him as he tried to punch me; or the time we were walking to a club and a man in a car wagged his tongue suggestively at me, and I, maddened, ran up to his car and kicked it until the light turned green—you pointing at the driver and telling him, *You're going to die;* or how you taught me to find a stick or a rock to carry on my walk home from work and how I used one once, against a car of teenagers—breaking their windshield before I ran like hell.

■ ■ ■

But—I must admit it—those aren't the times I think about. I think about the swollen silence between us that night on the subway, how the train screamed and shook and dragged itself along from stop to stop, noisily expressing everything we couldn't, or wouldn't. I think about how everything lodged itself in my eyes: dust, anger, tears. From time to time I could feel you looking at me and then away, but I, sitting by the door as it hissed open and shut, wouldn't look at you. Instead I watched a man across from me, who was idly playing with a bottle, shredding first the paper bag, then the bottle's label. I saw him without seeing—his shiny, porous skin, how his long hair didn't cover his scalp, how his mustache curled inside his mouth. When he looked back at me, I shifted my gaze automatically, staring at the advertisement above his head for a sad-eyed lawyer, with a telephone number stamped across his forehead in purple ink.

■ ■ ■

He got up and stood, swaying against the train's rhythm, close to me, close to the exit. I pulled myself tighter into myself, but only a little. I didn't want to seem scared. I didn't want to cuddle next to you, sitting so comforting and solid and infuriating next to me.

■ ■ ■

He said to me, menacing, *Whatchu looking at?*

You looked up. I stared at my boots, at the strips of damp newspaper on the floor, flattening my tongue inside my mouth.

He said again, *Whatchu looking at,* and then, wrapping his hand around the pole next to me so that I could see his neatly trimmed fingernails, *Dyke bitch?* He asked this in a singsong voice and leaned closer to me.

I wouldn't shrink away. (Not from him, not near you.) I looked up into his sunken face, into his bland, blue eyes, and I smelled adrenaline, that sweet-salt smell deep inside my nose. I told him, *Nothing.* I flicked my eyes over him and away, and repeated, *Nothing at all.*

You didn't say anything, though I was waiting for your arm to rise up, protective. No, you sat as still as a stranger. I bent my neck and examined my folded hands, listening to the doors swish open. I thought you were watching him, and that made me feel safe. I heard him get off—but no, you said later—you saw him stop. You told me later how he held the door open with his foot, how he turned and lunged toward me. You saw the bottle sliding over my head with that sudden splintering crash and you heard him screaming and you saw his lips turn back. You showed me later, and I saw it in your face. I saw it there.

■ ■ ■

Once a friend mimed a monster for me. She was an actress and she was doing it to further some other point in the conversation, to tell a story that I don't remember now. She pulled her hands in front of her face, making it seem as though her hands were pulling her features down into a contorted droop, a snarl of skin and teeth and eyes. Then, one moment later, she pulled her hand back up and was herself again. I felt such relief to see her old face back. I hadn't even known how disturbed I'd been, until I saw her regular self, smooth and upright and easy. When she resumed her conversation, I had to sit on my hands, resisting an urge to kiss her and hold her in my arms like a child and never let the monster come back.

■ ■ ■

Before you leave in the morning for work, so early, you part my sleep with questions—*do you need anything?* you ask me.

I shove a hand into the air. *I don't need you, I don't want you,* my hands say, urgently, but neither of us know that language.

When I come home at night you dance up from the TV set, your bright hair bent in wild angles from lying down so long, and squeeze me into your circle of light and I tell myself I'm where I want to be.

■ ■ ■

It's only when we get to bed and we peel off our clothes and shiver against each other and press our lips, like silent compliments, against each other's chests, that I begin again to blame you. Did I blame you right after it happened? Did I wonder as I lay toppled on the floor, drooling and bleeding against a gritty newspaper, why you left me for an elongated moment to scream, frenzied, after him? Did I wonder why you didn't ask anyone for help instead of holding me to you, fiercely picking glass from my head, and wiping roughly at my face; did I wonder, when we got to our stop, why you forced me to get up, to walk home in the dark, lurching inside my sobs and holding onto you?

I was scared, you told me later. You trusted no one. You left me alone only to call my best friend, who hung up the phone and called an ambulance. You didn't want to let the driver in, but at last pried open the door and let them clean and bandage me, right there in the bed, before they took me to the hospital, refusing you passage because you weren't family. To come see me, you had to go back to that same subway stop and wait again for that same train.

At the time, I didn't know where you were. All my thoughts shook as I lay in the jostling ambulance. The cheerful technician bent over me, gold teeth gleaming, breath garlicky in my face, and asked me jocular questions, laughing at my sloppy replies. The world became too shiny and slippery to hold onto. The technician's face was too close and, as he began to wrinkle and dip, he leaned even closer, looking anxious. The light was too sharp, the thick disinfectant smell too stinging—and then the technician disappeared from view. He was replaced with you, your difficult face. I knew you'd be there when I woke up, and you were. You looked rinsed out, but I didn't look at you much. I just stared, loosely, at the white hospital sheets.

It was my own private theater, replaying that breath of time you watched him stop the train doors and then turn. What, I wanted to know, were you thinking when you watched him slam that bottle on the top of my head? Did you feel a curious detachment, watching someone hit me in a way that you knew you never could? *Just tell me,* I thought, *I want to know.* Did you feel any envy watching him haul out that hate inside of him and shatter it on top of me?

Before he released the train door he spat—once at you and once at me. You, returning from your near pursuit, put your arms around me and held me against your body—while I scratched over and over at my face where his spit had landed. No one else on the train would come near us. You rocked me in your arms, crying small, bare tears. With one hand you picked off the glass and wiped the spit and blood from my face. You let the tears dry like a sheet of clear plastic on your cheeks. You said, *I'm sorry, I'm sorry,* and I mumbled, thickly, *Baby, it's not your fault, stop,* and at the time, I meant it. But afterward, when I opened my eyes and looked at you, I saw only a stranger—the same stranger my friend had become right as the monster was leaving her—right before she became herself again. Lying in your arms, the only thing I wanted, as though I'd never wanted anything before, was to have all of you back.

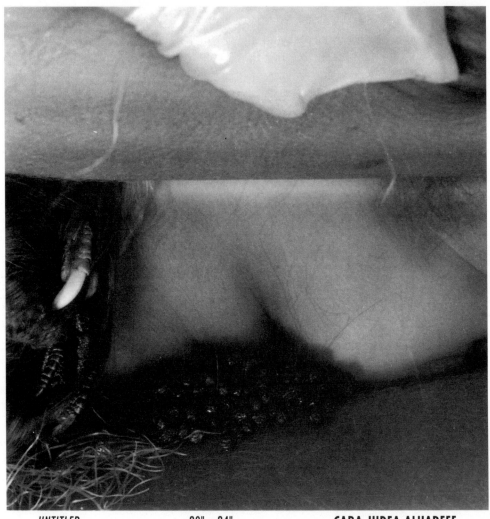

UNTITLED 20" x 24" **CARA JUDEA ALHADEFF**
color photo

In August 1992, my mother was (mis)diagnosed with a form of acute leuke-
mia. Although I began taking photographs seriously one year before my
mother's diagnosis, witnessing and participating in her experience has led me
to a more profound understanding of what compels me to photograph.

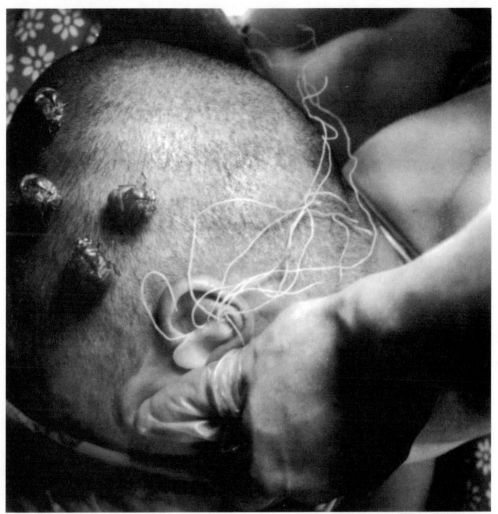

UNTITLED 20" x 24" **CARA JUDEA ALHADEFF**
color photo

I see my mother's relationship to her "health disorder" as a metaphor for the possibilities of transforming what is institutionally and socially perceived as vulnerability...like my photographs, this heightened state of awareness affirms the precarious balancing act of continually negotiating our desires and our intuitive understandings of how our bodies function, and the social norms which construct the latter.

not my teenage dream

i am not what i thought i'd be, but i'm as close as a girl like me ever got.

at age eight, my life's goal was to be a teenager.
this meant:
breakdancing/asymmetrical haircuts/boyfriends&gangs....
the movie "grease" changed my life forever. it taught me *cool*, taught me rebel and image. cyndi lauper taught me to be a non-conformist. all this combined made me wanna be the cool outcast who everybody looked up to. i wanted a leather jacket, fishnet tights, to be the tough hard-ass vixen who all the boys feared and wanted. my life's goals have changed but i still cling to the teenager in me.
wild and crazy.
trying to live my life like it's a movie
line up against the chain-link fence, bend our knees in time to "american woman" on the radio, smoke our cigarettes. i'll pretend i'm about to watch my boyfriend die in a game of chicken, though really i'm just waiting to go go-cart riding, and there's no boyfriend to speak of.

i took forty-eight hours coming into this world, born with a big blue bruise on my forehead, the doctor said "gotta fucked up leg, and she's probably blind and retarded."
the first thing i ever did was prove myself.
i looked into papa's eyes and he knew.
i was born on a tennessee commune, to non-conformist parents who eventually went back to their middle-class roots, the last of eight babies born within a year, i was the one who sat aside and watched, wore a funny shoe.

i'll admit it, i'm obsessed w/ glamour.
i'm trying to impress you. i wear silver eyeshadow for a reason.

i'm looking for a different kind of glamour, which is *my* kind of glamour. you know, the glamour of the fat jewish cripple girl who talks about herself incessantly and falls in love with all her girlfriends. i do wear fishnets now, i sing real pretty, wear fancy eye makeup when i feel up to it, or lounge around my apartment all day in my floor-length silver nightgown.

when i was fourteen, a pseudo-depressed goth rocker w/ too much black eye makeup and dyed black hair, i told my friend marcel,
"i wanna change the world."
i didn't know what that meant really, but i really meant it. i had tears in my eyes.
in my head i knew it was cuz there were too many people suffering, but i didn't know where to make the connections, where to start the process of change. marcel said,
"we should kill all the rich people. except rich black people, cuz they deserve what they have."✷
to me that just sounded like more suffering, but maybe if i'd taken it as a metaphor i would've known where to start.

there's this thing called "x" that's trying to colonize the minds of my generation. it's a tool. it keeps us quiet, diverts our attention, makes us feel ineffective and incapable. it tells us that there is no beauty in life, nothing to live or fight for. it says we're lost and should accept that fate.
generation x is killing my instincts. generation x is killing the survivor in me. fuck it, i can't afford to buy into apathy.
i am not afraid to say i've had a hard life. most of the women i know have had hard lives. we breathe in self-hatred like oxygen, and when we're told to watch our calorie intake, we eat our self-hatred like gluttons.
we come from different places, poor, abused, taught to hate our bodies and our minds. we are trying to understand our experiences, finding the courage to trust ourselves as allies, to seek each other out.
we are learning:
things are not simple, not cut and dry, but there are enemies. name it what you want: the fucker/ The Man/ the system. most of us have been fighting the fucker all our lives. it's not a doomed fate. we are tracking his moves, antici-

pating and subverting. redefining ourselves in terms of community, self-worth, and struggle. in this struggle we find beauty, art, life, and meaning. we are not hollow.

it's a process:
last winter i got really depressed
felt like my whole life stemmed from horror and shame; became disillusioned and incapacitated. i cried a lot, felt unsafe even with friends, wondered what the hell i was doing and why i had to live in this body and this life.

i've spent my life developing this hip smart & talented personality cuz i needed something to prove i was real. to prove i wasn't like those other fat girls, those other cripples, the people we stare at on the bus and feel sorry for.

(pity could destroy me)
thing is, us fat cripple girls, we're tough. we gotta be. and when we finally see through that toughness, strip it away and look at the shit that's buried beneath it, it's like a fucking bulldozer. i mean, it'll knock you down.

and sometimes
well sometimes it feels easier to live a lie. to live in denial.
and there comes a time when i need to choose:
do i want what's easy, or what's real?

i am living in a country built on alleged freedoms and innumerable myths. any freedoms i am handed are at the expense of others. and vice versa. i am watching things get worse, watching the tension building. i know where i stand in this hierarchy.

but the system isn't as stable as it appears to be. i've seen things change: for example i've seen myself and my community start deconstructing the myths and lies of fat-hate, found allies around the world, and started digging out my own shame and self-contempt. i've found a safe space for myself and other fat people.

by politicizing my life, i am figuring out where i stand and what i'm capable of.
i am defining my goals.
and "changing the world" is coming much closer to home than it ever did when i was fourteen.

we have lofty goals.

we're fighting for the liberation and self-determination of all people.

but it's more than posturing and slogans. every day we're trying to do something concrete. my roommate is planting metaphorical bombs in safeway as we speak. we are planning. we are putting plans into action. we are artists and revolutionaries.

we are

in process,

doing what we can.

i was born into struggle. it can be overwhelming, but anyway i'm not sorry. it means that forgetting my goals just isn't an option. in this fight, i gotta stay focused, gotta work hard, gotta put myself on the line and learn to find trust. things don't come easy, but they do come.

things don't come easy, but hell, fuck easy. anything easy probably isn't worth it.

i'm glad i'm not my teenage dream,

cuz at least i know i'm real.

Wade's Hoggers

The name of my mother's bowling team.

"You have to know what a hogger is," she said.

I'm thinking pig. Fat pigs.
I'm thinking it's not funny to name a team "Hoggers."
I'm thinking of the time I was nearly suspended
from fourth grade
for fighting with a girl
who said my mother was fat.

I'm thinking of how careful my mother was
to take dainty steps
and walk slowly
so that the wind was not disturbed by her mass,
so that people didn't get pushed over
by her wake.

I'm thinking about her shock
at the obvious disgust of my father
as she grew larger after every child.

I'm thinking of tropical purple mu mus
sagging chairs,
stretched-out shoes.

I'm thinking about her heart getting squeezed
between her lungs.

I'm thinking about a photo of my mother at age four.
Her chubby, baby-fat face,

her hands hooked in the front by two plump fingers,
she is standing in front of her house.
To her left is a table, and a cake with four candles.
She's not smiling.

"What is a hogger, mom?" I ask.

"It digs up potatoes. It's a farm tool."

"Oh," I say.

I'm thinking of Wade
hanging a framed photo of his champion Hoggers
on the wall of his shop.

I'm thinking of all the farmers who
will comment on the picture: a row of women in their fifties,
"Hoggers" stitched in pink across their chests.

I want to say, "Mom, eat the cake."

Victoria Told Me Her Secret

My father is suspicious of my wardrobe.
Guilty, my thick-soled shoes—
a militant line
at the bottom of my closet.

Practical shirts
with mannish collars and tails
swing on plastic hangers
above the shoes.

Across a rack of denim
or khaki trousers,
a row of brimmed caps,
and nearby an unflattering
red and black checkered robe.

He never says so, but I suspect
my father thinks
that I have a false bottom in my chest of drawers
where I store
my dominatrix suit, my whip,
and sculpted silicone items.

During a long-distance conversation
he compares me to videos
he has seen
of two or more women
moaning and rolling
like cats in heat
tonguing the air
pretending to hurt
or to please each other.

He admits that many men
share this fantasy.

While he expounds on this
my body turns plastic and
welds to the phone.

I wish he were here in person
so I could deck him
right out of his shoes.
I'd pull out the lifts
he walks on to look taller than
hot pink California girls
and force him to wear his new wife's lingerie
that cuts and scratches
the genitals.

I would pull out his stash of sex toys
and line them up like bowling trophies.

I'd send him running
from his own secrets
but he'd find
that wearing stilettos impedes him,
and the secrets
catch up,
tackle,
and deep kiss him
red hair and lipstick everywhere,
ramming their tongues down his throat
just the way he
doesn't
like it.

My Breasts: Two Views

I.
You got small, stubborn breasts, a man
once told me, trying to squish them together
the way men do. He was right: as far
apart from each other as possible, the nipples

jutting in different directions, my breasts
are like the chins of sisters

who aren't speaking, but are
forced to sit together on the same couch.
A portrait of estrangement clings

to my chest—from that day on
making clear my position
on rough-handed men.

II.
Your breasts are beautiful, a woman
tells me, after we've lost both our shirts
and our shyness. So are hers, flowing down

her body like heavy rain. When we kiss, I feel
them against mine; they hover and draw
close, like moths to flames. No—like moths

to moths, flames to flames. Childless mothers
nursing one another, something more necessary
than milk
is exchanged in this dark room
we fill with the smell of sun.

excerpt from the law school mailbox sex poems

for m

11 march
dr. meyer asked me today what is going on in my life what happened this week and i felt like my glow was filling the room like your scent was emanating from me your breath still in my ear he wanted to know what i was attracted to what you aroused in me but where was i to begin even if i restricted myself to last night where was i supposed to begin with your casual kisses in the kitchen or your repeated apologies for not being ready when i wanted to watch you lick the honey off the spoon split the outside of the onion without scratching the interior crush the garlic with the flat of the knife i mean i was aroused by the way your eyes lit up when you talked about tax law and the way you recreated a recipe with only the remembered taste and at dinner knees touching discussing past loves of boys women motorcycles i loved the image of you on a harley no helmet your hair in tangles for me to work through with my fingers and afterwards the weight of your head in my lap touching your face your neck watching your face your eyes close moving on top of you pressing my body against every inch of yours licking all of the ridges and grooves of your teeth kissing you deep and hard until our teeth collided and you asked me what i wanted you asked me what would turn me on but i was turned on i was turned on by your whisper by the way you straddled me rose above me barechested the street light coming in from behind and i couldn't tell you what aroused me i couldn't even tell you because i was underground warm and safe and you were an earthquake above me through me and i want to make you tremor until you come i want to feel the vibrations from the inside i want to be on the inside i want your wetness on my thigh my fingers my tongue i want to make you collapse on top of me i mean i loved the way you coaxed it out of me yanked it out of me you said *you can trust me* and i trusted you i let go i cried out i came three times fully clothed laughing in amazement each time i whispered *don't leave me in a week* you said *don't worry*

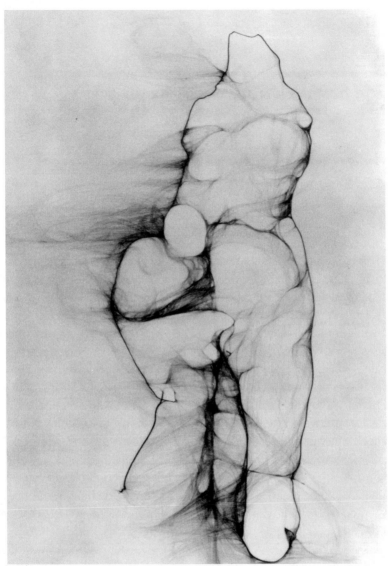

UNTITLED, OCTOBER 1993   32" x 40"   **DOROTHY EILEEN GOODE**
pencil

My work is a descent into sickness. It probes the places of refuge: the holes cut for the purpose of hiding both mind and body in this elusive mobility of identity. It is about sex and the self-destructive. It attempts to locate the necessity in the intolerable, and the beauty in how one must respond to the intolerable.

NIGHTGOWN   24" x 36"   **LESLIE RIIBE**
color photo

"Nightgown" is one photograph of a larger, collaborative project with my mother in which we played "let's pretend Mom's a performance artist." I documented this process, while she posed as B-movie monster, boxer, and Catholic schoolgirl. Within this mimicry of art, a true parallel piece of work emerges.

I WEAR YOUR RING　　　　24" x 32"　　　　**ANDREA NICOLICH**
oil on watercolor paper

My work is everything that I am.
There are no right or wrong meanings.
It is not political nor religious.
It's not about world news and it's not meant to offend.
It is just what it is—who I am. Emotional. Powerful. Feminine. Solitary. Erotic.
Violent. Sometimes disturbing. Always honest.

The Wings

When they were married in the Salt Lake Temple, she saw how it would be after she died, in the resurrection. Marriage was a dry run for immortality, a message from God telling them what it would be like. Wing-back chairs, crystal-and-gold chandeliers, oak, marble, stained glass letting in the daylight, beige walls with paintings of Christ beckoning his rag-clad followers, ceilings so high she could hardly see them. She thought of God in the spaces between the walls, airy, just beyond what she could see, so big He filled the entire place, or standing just behind her, vanishing when she turned. When she and her husband were married, they were covered in white up to their necks, and all their guests were covered in white. The temple was even covered in white. Her husband stood in the inmost room, the holiest, loveliest, right there next to God's heart, she thought, separated from her by a curtain, and then he pulled her in. This is how it would be.

On Sunday morning, oh, it was always so hard to get everyone in order. The boys wouldn't be dressed, or they would dress in nice shirts and pajama bottoms, or they would not have remembered to brush their teeth until they were almost out the door. She had to find the right dress, remember what she'd worn all those last Sundays, find some pantyhose that matched. Her husband, though, was always there, right on time, perfect. Once they got to church, they sat in the fifth row. There were always the same number of songs before the Sacrament, three. The bishop told them what was going on in the ward, like a holy news reporter. Then they took the Sacrament, then different people (it didn't matter who) talked about the Lord. There at church everyone knew what to do. The little one was even old enough not to bang his legs against the seat.

On Sunday night, this particular Sunday night, she was satisfied. Things went as planned. The chicken dinner—chicken baked in mushroom sauce and potatoes whipped in her blue mixing bowl—went as planned. The children behaved. On nights like this, she didn't go up on the rooftop. She offered herself up to her husband just like she offered up her sins to God, and then she slept the whole night long. She never woke up once, not even to go to the bathroom.

On Monday morning after everyone had left, she sat on the living room couch with a cup of honey tea. Everyone was where they were supposed to be: at school, at work. The boys would come home for lunch and she would make them split pea soup and tuna fish sandwiches. For dinner it would be lasagna; she'd have to start that early.

In between the lunch and dinner, though, she wasn't sure what would happen. That was bad, three hours where anything might happen. But it would be fine; she'd read her scriptures, the Book of Mormon, the part where Alma says to his people that Christ can never vary from what's right, that Christ's course is one eternal round. Yes, everything would be all right.

That night she turned on the electric heater and waited for her soft husband to come to bed. She hoped he wouldn't want anything and when he kissed her she turned away. When he lay back down, she put her arm around his body and kissed his shoulder. Good night, she said.

Sometimes, like tonight, when she couldn't sleep, she would open the window and go out to the roof. Part of the roof, just for decoration, slanted just past her window; she would climb up that part like a cat, with her bare feet and her hands. She would go up partway to the top, where the roof narrowed to a point, staying on just by using the friction between her body and the red roof tile. Or she might climb toward the back of the house, where the roof flattened out. There, it was covered with sticky black tar. Afterward, when she came back, her hands and feet would be gritty with bits of red roof tile and sometimes sticky with black tar, and she'd get bits of tar or red tile on her white sheets. But before that happened she could feel the cool air and look at the darkness; she could feel how nighttime felt without her husband.

In the morning she had things to do. After breakfast there were spots of blackberry jam on the table that she had to wipe off, hope they wouldn't stain. A drawer that could be organized. In a few days she would have to make cookies for the ward party because it was her turn. She could go to the grocery store today, especially since her husband was out of shaving cream and they were a little low on catsup.

At night he asked her, Why don't you want to do it, and she said, I won't mind, really. It was just not important for her. Not interesting. She would rather feel the wisps of his chest hair with her fingers, have his arm protecting her back. She was willing enough, though, and when they finished she reached for a roll of toilet paper to clean it all up, then she went into the bathroom and sat on the toilet, letting it drip away from her. This had to be better than douches, because douches just push it up farther. Not that she didn't want any more babies, oh no, because she did. Really she did.

When she came back to bed she watched him sleep, because he was beautiful. She smelled the sweet smell of Drakkar on his neck. She wondered what she would smell like wearing Rose Petal, and would it clash with his cologne? She put her head down on the pillow and tried to relax, breathing in and out with her chest, then her abdomen, then her sides. She stared at the wall. Then she saw a puff of white out the window.

Who are you? she called, and when nothing answered she got up and opened the window, and the puff flew away to a tree in the neighbor's yard. She climbed out onto the roof for a better look, and the puff of white flew behind her house, so she had to climb all the way to the top of the roof, standing up and holding onto the pointed edge with her hands. She saw long red hair, softly clawed feet, wings that folded perfectly into the body. Come back, she said, and she almost lost her balance trying to see the angel's face. But the angel didn't pay any attention, just lifted its clawed foot to its mouth and nibbled on it. Then it unfurled its wings, each of them six feet long, and flew off toward the south.

In the morning she didn't want a bubble bath but she wanted her honey tea. She wanted to call Sister Mortensen but she didn't. She thought she might want to make the cookies that day instead of the day after, so she got out the butter and nutmeg and milk and eggs and sugar and flour and put it all in a mixing bowl, but then she looked closely and noticed there were bugs crawling around in the flour, and she had to take everything outside and dump it in the garbage. She hosed the bowl down before she brought it back in the house, but even so she was a little worried that the bugs might have crawled someplace, so she got out the bleach and disinfected the floors and then the cabinet. By the time that was done the boys were home, so she didn't have any time to go to the store and get more flour. Butter too, she'd used up most of the butter.

At dinner she made up for not baking cookies like she should have by getting a pound cake out of the freezer and serving it after the spaghetti casserole. Really, they didn't go together, but no one seemed to mind. In bed her husband seemed happier than ever, so she lay there and thought about the scriptures. Her body was a temple, not to be defiled by passionate thoughts or actions or anything else—dirty words, coffee, wine. In real life you had to have a slip of paper, signed by your bishop, in order to go into the temple. Everyone protected the temple. But your body had nobody to protect it but you.

After he was asleep she had an idea, and she went downstairs to get a bit of leftover pound cake. She went back upstairs to the bedroom window, opened it, held the pound cake out at arm's reach. The angel had been hovering in the next yard, and it circled close, closer, and looked at the pound cake with its small black eyes, but would not take it. She put the pound cake on the roof and shut the window and watched. The angel flew closer and closer until she could see its body, saw that it had tattoos on its legs, pink flowers circling green dragons the way the tattoos circled the angel's legs. Then the angel grabbed the pound cake with its clawed foot and flew away.

Night after night it was like that. The angel would fly closer and closer, until the woman could sit on top of the roof and hold the food (a bit of apple, a piece of bread, who knows what angels like best?) away from her body, and the angel would come. She could see parts of the naked angel, enough to know it was a woman, but she would look away from those parts, ashamed, down to the tattooed legs or up at the dirty white wings. She grabbed at the wings once, not knowing why, but the angel backed off the edge of the roof and rose high above her. The angel did not come back that night.

Days the woman could not seem to do anything after everyone had left, so she went back to bed and watched the red digits on her alarm clock shift. Things went undone: crumbs of toast sat on the carpet and were taken away by ants, lunches didn't get ready in time, the toy Count from Sesame Street lay on the kitchen floor for two days before she noticed him and put him back in his Sesame Street house. Her husband pretended not to notice, figuring, she thought, it was that time of the month. But all that time, she was planning. She would catch the angel by its tattooed legs and *make* her carry her to where the angels go. Yes, and she would carry a bag of rice, dyed green, and drop it on the way so she could find the angel's home again in the morning, after everyone had left.

One night she stood on the tarred part of the roof and offered the angel, who was crouching in a tree, some raisins. The angel moved toward the woman and opened her wings, looking as if she would take hold of the woman with them and pull her toward her chest. Then the woman saw the tattoos weren't just on the angel's legs, but climbed up the sides of her body and spread out toward her wings. The woman touched the angel on her soft stomach, in the safe place between the pubic hair and the breasts, and the angel folded in on herself like a little piece of origami. Then the woman stroked the soft wings, smoothing the feathers that were sticking out awkwardly, flicking away the white dandruffy bits of dead skin. The angel opened her wings a little and made a soft bird cry. The woman offered her raisins again, but the angel didn't take them. She just watched the woman for a while, smelling sweaty and creamy and nicely sour, then moved her head back and forth the way birds do when they are about to fly, and beat her wide wings at the air until she lifted up.

The woman wanted to do that, too. She spread her arms but they were not wings, and they did not lift her up. She walked to the side of her roof and wondered for a minute what would happen if she walked right off the edge. Then she thought, in the morning they would find me and what would they think? Possessed by demons. Yes, that was it. There was once a bishop who wanted to know more about the occult, who studied Church books and then academic books and finally the books written by people who loved the devil, until one day he lifted three feet off the floor of the dining room and started banging his head on the ceiling. His wife called a man in the Stake Presidency who called a man in the Quorum of the Twelve, who came over and prayed softly to the Lord for an hour until the man fell to the floor, having learned his lesson. Who sells eternity to get a toy?

She scooted down the roof and climbed back in the window. The grains of roof tile fell off her feet onto the floor, and she left them there when she got back into bed. She rolled her husband's body over onto hers, and he said, Huh? She tried to pray but how could she, there was nothing to say if she wasn't going to say she was sorry. Then she went to sleep. She dreamed of dark holes that make you disappear if you touch them. She dreamed she was disappearing.

In the morning the can opener didn't work; every time she tried to use it the detachable attachment came off, and she couldn't make any tuna fish. The boys had to have peanut butter for lunch instead. When she walked by the broom closet, the little whoosh of wind she made caught the broom and it fell down, clackety-clack-bang. A candle fell out of her hand and rolled into the fireplace, got covered with ashes. The dishwasher leaked and when she pulled out the lower rack to take a look she found a lump of seaweed in it: how did seaweed get in her house? It was the house, yes, it had to be the house against her. It didn't like her on its roof? She didn't know. Or maybe it was what she knew in the back of her head, that she couldn't have both things, the angel and the perfect house. She could only have one or the other.

Saturday night she lay in bed and tried to sleep. When she shut her eyes, a voice like the man on television earlier that night told her about the New World snowy egret, its long neck and long legs, the way male and female together cared for the young, how millinery had nearly wiped it out. She could feel her husband pawing at her with fuzzy bear hands and she turned toward him, but in her half-sleep she was still there, with the snowy egret. Afterward she got up and sat on the toilet while the semen leaked out, and then she went back to bed and tried to sleep, tried to sleep, until she couldn't stand it and she *had* to go out onto the roof with the peeled orange she had by the bed-side (so yes, she had planned it, she had to say that, she was guilty of mean-ing to do it) and wait for the angel. When the angel finally came, she fed her the way she would feed a lover, the way her husband fed her cream puffs once until she laughed and turned her head away. She fed her slice by slice, not pulling her hand away until the angel's wet lips touched her fingers. Then she stroked the feathers on the angel's wings, and she touched the inky tattoo on her thigh to feel whether the skin was smooth or rough. She could feel (oh so lightly) the outline of leaves on the angel's legs, and she could smell (only just barely) flowers, like lilies.

When she went back to bed she stroked her husband's leg to see if it felt like the angel's, but it was just hairy. She rubbed the hairs on his thigh and felt them with her finger pads. Then she had to feel his penis; that would be softer, smoother, and it was. When she cupped it in her hand, she felt it start to grow, and she started rubbing and squeezing it the way she saw him do when he thought she was asleep. She felt tremendous, ticklish, as if she were as big as an airplane or rolling through dandelions. Her whole body itched. By the time he woke up she was already on top of him, and by the time they were done she had licked, bitten just as much as he.

On Sunday morning she panicked when she woke up, as if someone were dying. Her heart beat fast, it must have been 140 beats a minute, until she checked to see that her husband and boys were all there. Then she opened her closet door and the bar that held all the clothes hangers fell, everything crashing to the ground. She shut the door, quick, but nobody came to yell at her and she opened it again and picked out a dress. Her husband could fix the bar on Monday but until then all her clothes would have to be on the floor. Dust would settle on them, bugs would crawl over them.

Later, when she cracked open an egg to make breakfast, a chick popped out, said Cheep, and fell onto the counter, dead. She wanted to sit down then, quit, cry, but she couldn't let the boys see the chick. She took it outside to give it a proper burial, and when she got back in the house her dress had somehow gotten dirt on it.

But the husband and the boys, they were spotless. After breakfast they all got in the car and drove to church. They sat down and then Sister Mortensen sat down with her five little girls, all of them wearing the dresses Sister Mortensen had sewn, lavendar floral prints with puffy sleeves. She'd have sewn dresses for her girls, too, only she didn't have girls, she had boys. She brushed another bit of dirt off her own dress, bought at a store in the mall. And then the other thing was, how would she have found the time for all that sewing? She noticed a bit of slime near the hem of her dress, probably from the chick. She didn't know why she hadn't changed into another dress.

When they passed the Sacrament around, she didn't take it, even though Sister Mortensen was watching. Next week she would take it; she'd shut the blind and not go near the angel, not once.

After church she asked the bishop if they could talk, and they went into his office. She didn't know how she could say to him, I have been, night after night, going up to my roof for love of an angel. In the end she said, I desire a woman. He wanted to know, Who, does she reciprocate, and she couldn't say. Have you acted on it, he said, and she said, No. Keep your scriptures nearby, he said, hold them close to your heart. This is grave but with the help of the Lord we will prevail. The bishop's forehead wrinkled and she left the room, embarrassed.

That evening her husband came back from going to the temple (or so he said), and something wasn't right; he had a funny glow like he'd had his face near a fire. He grinned with all his teeth and held the oldest boy upside down by his legs, to shake out all the yellow, he said laughing, and the oldest boy laughed, too. The boy struggled and then fell on the ground with a bang, but then he sat up again and untied her husband's shoelaces. I have a present, her husband said, and he took saltwater taffy out of his pockets to give to them.

I have a present for you, too, he said to her later, when they were in the bedroom, and he gave it to her: a purple nylon leotard with a hole between the legs, black panties, and a black dress that looked as though it had been shrunk. Oh, she said. Put them on, he said. Oh, she said. Do I take off the garments? she said. Is that against the rules? and he rubbed his hand all through her hair and down her neck, so it tingled and she had to pull away. She could put the leotard on, and the panties, but the dress was so tight he had to help her pull it over her shoulders, and he had to zip up the zipper. It was long and sleek and dark.

Turn around for me, he said, smiling. Should I? she said. Sure, he said. She spun around in her stocking feet. She didn't feel holy enough. When he pulled her toward the bed she said, Let's sleep with the blind shut, I can't sleep with it open. She pulled the covers up over her body and her black dress like a turtle and shut her eyes. She thought holy thoughts, and half fell asleep. After he had finished and put her black panties back on she woke up a little and watched the ceiling, which spinned. Spun. She was not going to open the blinds, she was not going to go out there, that was that. Final. She'd wake him up first, tell him she wanted it, before she would go out there again. If she went out, would it all spin, the stars, the moon, or would it be the house spinning under her? She was not going to go out. In the morning, at six-fifty, she would wake up, make lunches, make orange juice from concentrate. Little glasses for her and the children, a big glass for her husband. By seven-thirty they would all be gone. Not going out. Then she would sit around reading her scriptures. She was not going out. Or maybe there wouldn't be time for that; she'd have to take a shower and clean the house before ten, when she had to meet with Sister Jensen to plan out the songs for the next Sunday. Then she remembered what she was wearing, and she meant to take it all off and put her garments back on, but instead, feeling the way the black panties pushed into her skin, she moved her legs a little to make the panties push even better. She fell asleep and woke up once, when she thought she heard the sad sound of claws at the window.

In the morning the alarm didn't go off. Her husband had to go to work without shaving, dirty-chinned, and then the younger boy hit the older boy on the cheek, hard, and how could she send him to school with a bruise? What would they think? Then she went back to bed, forgot all about Sister Jensen and when Sister Jensen came all she could find to wear was a cotton dress with a rip down the side, held closed by a safety pin. Tattered. The day was tattered. Wouldn't it be getting better, though? Wouldn't the house calm down, now that she was done with the angel?

That night she had no mushroom sauce, so she tried to use tomato sauce instead. The chicken came out looking bloody, with loose clumps of tomato looking like raw bits of skin. Poor carcass, her son said. Her husband ate, maybe to be kind, maybe thinking he would be rewarded later, ha! As soon as she thought that, she thought, I should not be thinking that about him, poor thing.

All the men in her life fidgeted after dinner. The younger boy ran his train around the living room carpet, saying vrr-r-rr, and the older boy switched the television set on and off. Her husband unbuttoned his pants and walked from room to room, Looking for something, he said every time she asked. She went upstairs and took off everything for him, even the garments, and put on a T-shirt nightgown, but by the time he finally sent the boys to bed and came upstairs she was asleep, the blankets wrapped tightly against her body. In her dreams, giant headless chickens flew at her, enraged. Then she thought she felt her husband reaching for her in the dark, and after that, when she thought perhaps he was still working at it, she thought she heard the pitter-patter of her son's footsteps. Laughing in whispers, just outside the door, listening to them. She started awake; she rolled over to touch her husband and he was not there. Where was he? In the bathroom? She waited but she didn't hear anything. She got up and then she thought, the roof.

She opened the window and climbed up the grainy red tile, but no one was there. Then she heard sounds, like soft breathing and touching. She climbed toward the back of the house, where the black tar was, and no one was there. It was cold, and she tried to cover herself better with her T-shirt nightgown, but a bit of wind came and exposed her pubic hair. Suddenly she thought—and why hadn't she ever thought this before?—that someone could see her, out there on the roof! She hurried back toward the tile, nearly falling off the roof, and clambered up it, then down again toward the bedroom window. But in her way, blocking the window, there was the angel, half-sitting, half-lying, and facing her husband, who was touching her between her legs with his hand. He couldn't! They couldn't! Oh, but didn't she deserve it, such a bad wife, not staying in the house like an ordinary woman but having to come out to the roof every night and, she had to admit, she wanted to do what her husband was doing. It was her fault. She sat down on the roof and the angel looked up at her (probably seeing, like all the neighbors might have seen, those vile pubic hairs), but the woman had to look away so she wouldn't see the places her husband was touching. She would just wait until they were done; that was all.

But she couldn't. The wind snuck in through the holes in the fabric of the tee shirt nightgown, licking her nipples, no matter how tightly she crossed her arms in front of them, and she knew the Lord was looking down on her, shaking his head. And something was coming inside of her, slow like a steamroller, but coming steadily, until she knew what it was. It was what Jesus did when he saw the money-changers. She stood up and ran toward the angel, shouting, Shoo! so that the angel lost her balance and toppled off the roof. She opened her wings just before she reached the ground, and then made a lonely wail and flew away. She flew south without looking back, until she was just a dot in the sky.

Then the woman climbed back in through the window, put on her garments, and went straight to bed, lying stiff and still when her husband followed. In the morning it would be all right again; yes, it had to be. She'd have sheets to wash, breakfasts and lunches to make. In the morning she'd get up, she'd have her honey tea, she'd take her bubble bath, she'd go to the store and buy some more light bulbs to replace the ones that had burned out in the kitchen.

UNTITLED　　　　　14" x 14"　　　　　**MONICA NUVAMSA**
　　　　　　　　　　pen & ink

To me, my art is more than just pictures. It is my meditation and my history. All my experience, thought, and feeling enter each line that is put on paper by my hand. Throughout history, Indian women have struggled to create artistic work of talent and skill as well as reflect a foundation of family values and creative tradition. These struggles provide me with motivation for my own artwork. My visual meditation of my culture and of my family reminds me to remain focused on the entire picture at hand which is our world environment, spirituality, and harmony. This is my path and my role in the life my culture refers to as being in the fourth world.

Trinity

The white sands of New Mexico
reflect light over the continental divide
but when you stand on them (a blankness
visible from space), the grains absorb
the sun like they swallow the whispers
of dead cottonwood leaves and
the screams of turbine engines.

Back in this Mormon town named
for a Catholic saint, bulldozers
pile red dirt alongside the road.
It smells like blood, like my dream
of eyeless animals dragging
across the desert to die
under creosote, under mesquite.

It ends with the flash at Trinity,
John Donne reciting "Batter my heart,
three-personed God" as the grains fuse
into a new jade-colored gem.
They backfilled the impact crater
and told us it was a routine munitions test
in this land of wind made visible.

Reviews

BECKY RODIA

GIRL SOLDIER. Denise Duhamel, Garden Street Press, PO Box 1231, Truro, MA 02666, 1996, 61 pages, $13 paper.

Denise Duhamel's third full-length collection of poems, *Girl Soldier,* chronicles a search for female identity. From Girl Scouts bonding in a "Human Knot" to Duhamel's mother trying to savor a solitary swim, each woman in the book is a girl soldier struggling toward a greater understanding of herself, her connection to other women, and her place in the world. Duhamel's characteristic humor eases but never trivializes the rigor of the crusade. Even when she laughs at herself, which is often, the feeling is that she's really laughing *with* herself; her idiosyncrasies and shortcomings are *hers,* and laughter is a way of accepting them.

The book is permeated with a sense of guilt. *I learned to masturbate late, / in my mid-twenties, with a self-help book.* So begins "Whole," the book's opening poem. With candid hindsight, the speaker recalls her kindergarten fear of learning to *tumble,* while the other girls in class *lined up to do it again and again.* The speaker's fear sets her apart; she is a late bloomer *half-abandon[ing her]self to death* while others are *having orgasms in public.* Compared to these sexually comfortable people, the speaker is imperfect, less than whole.

"Shame" chronicles several moments of public embarrassment in the speaker's life and intersperses them with the private embarrassments endured at her gynecologist's office. At the poem's end we learn the speaker was once raped, and we understand that this particular victimization has made her feel as though *everyone* singles her out for blame.

Many poems in *Girl Soldier* focus on the narrator's mother, who is another source of guilt. In "From the Shore," the mother swims farther and farther out, leaving the narrator and her sister to wonder: *Had we dragged mud from the sand castle to the blanket / or sung too loud or fought with each other?* The mother's apparent departure leaves the children wondering what they did to upset the *wet monster* who only returns when another mother-figure demands it: *get back on shore // to take care of your daughters.* The mother returns, grumbling *Can't I have one goddamn minute alone?*—reinforcing the girls' guilt. In a prose poem, "The Threat," the mother throws the narrator's sister out of the house, then asks the narrator to take sides: *my mother wouldn't let me open the door to let my sister back in... she was cold rubbing her sleeves a mug of coffee in her hand and I had to decide she said I had to decide right then.*

The mother's girl-soldier search for self is inextricable from her relationship with her children. "My Mother Is A Big White Stove" equates the mother with practical, utilitarian things: food, bowls, a car, a freezer, pots, and a stove. In "Summer," the mother is a sleepy, lounging animal, a *bear* who has surely *eaten* the missing father. This mother is defined by her children; even when she tries to make time for herself, they leave no room for *one goddamn minute alone.*

Duhamel's sense of self and humor at times effectively defy any feelings of guilt, as in "Witches," a poem about deception. The narrator is cast as Glinda the Good Witch in her high school's production of "The Wizard of Oz" not because she is good, but because she has *the right hair— / big puffy blond curls*. Throughout the poem, *bad witches* deceive good women for use in evil deeds. The mother appears again, a bad witch who, like the narrator, resembles a good witch: *We took a lot of time in the morning to get our hair right*. The duality is intentionally confusing—bad witches want to appear good to unsuspecting victims—but it also confuses the witches themselves; they can't answer Glinda's question—*Are you a good witch or a bad witch?...*—which serves as the poem's epigraph. The narrator admits: *At home I called my mother a witch / when I was mad, rather than when I loved her.... We were witches then with no idea that we were*. She knows that she and her mother are somehow the same—equally hateful or lovable, bad or good, always trying to trick the other into serving her purposes. Although the mother is terrifying—a D&C starts her blood *pouring,* pills make her *angry, then sleepy*—the narrator adds a note of pity to these details. Acknowledging her mother as an equal is a way of forgiving her.

One of the final poems in *Girl Soldier* explores women's sexual history and continued liberation. "Ortho-Novum 777" begins with contemplation of the *pastel peaches and greens* of birth-control pills and proceeds to poke playful fun at past myths about contraception and conception: *Mini-fetuses, it was once thought, / lived in the sperm, intact*. The poem celebrates women's ability to control their reproductive lives, and the ease and pleasure resulting from that control. The narrator wonders, *Who was the first woman to mark her cycle / on a calendar, ask her mate / to pull out before he came?* She feels a kinship to this pioneer in contraception and extends solidarity to all those like her: *The earth is round / and finite, pregnant. I stand with the women / who sing at its flat-bellied cliffs*.

The abundance of poems dealing with sex and the female body is appropriate—every woman must come to terms with her body as both ally and enemy; both sides are fully represented in *Girl Soldier,* and both sides strengthen women's search for collective and individual identities. The book's title poem expresses it perfectly:

> They're told alone they'd be naked and squashy,
> just ready for soup. But when they're reminded
> this is not true, girls feel a deep strength
> that has something to do with the earth.
> Vaginas from all countries make peace—
> the root of the word literally meaning sheath,
> a resting place for men and their swords.

DORA ALICIA RAMIREZ

HER WILD AMERICAN SELF. M. Evelina Galang, Coffee House Press, 27 North Fourth Street, Suite 400, St. Paul, MN 55401, 1996, 192 pages, $12.95 paper.

M. Evelina Galang's first book of twelve short stories, *Her Wild American Self,* is difficult to define as anything except American. Galang's characters take the reader to distant shores through the memories and experiences of Filipino American women who struggle to maintain their individuality in a society that simply categorizes them as "Asian."

Writing in the novella style of Sandra Cisneros , with the grace and fervor of an imaginative creator of fictive worlds, Galang pushes at the boundaries of culture, tradition, and sexuality while intermixing her own sense of a Filipino American's experiences in an unforgiving society. She captures the complexity of her many characters' intricate lives.

The voice of the tradition-bound woman, who has internalized obedience and feels she must obey her strict father in "Miss Teenage Sampaguita," reveals the connection that Filipino women have with their families and how, in return, they are treated and seen by their relatives. These traditions, which if rejected can lead to disownment by the family or disgrace by the community, are demonstrated by Millicent's submissiveness to her father. Galang creates an undercurrent of feminism among the younger generation of her women characters by allowing the reader to see that Millicent thrives on her personal desires. Millicent subverts her father's wishes by hiding those desires from him, and her goals redefine her view of Filipino culture and tradition.

In "Contravida," Lisa, a single, pregnant woman, is confronted by those same traditions that Millicent is beginning to break down. Lisa, an older aunt, confronts her family with what they consider a shameful, disheartening situation. She is stared at and shunned by many of her relatives but is able to overcome old traditions that her *Tita* Lina has carried with her. The simple action of *Tita* Lina placing her hand on Lisa's robust, pregnant stomach brings into focus for the reader realize the fact that, although *In [her] day, [they] never touched the mother's stomach,* the older generation is finally breaking some of those barriers that separate the Filipino family from the Filipino-American family.

One of the most captivating stories, which explores both the feminist and cultural sides of a woman's experiences, is the nerve-testing "Filming Sausage." This story captures the torn devotion of the Filipina Elena Romero, who knows only "American" life but is sexually harassed by an American male who sees only the "exotic." This brings to the reader's attention the existence of the notion of exoticism surrounding Asians in America:

> *Because there seem to be no lines, no walls, between the Japanese, Vietnamese, Koreans, Chinese and the Filipino, even you have to come to believe you are no different than the rest. The look-alike women, the beautiful women. The women of the Orient.*

Galang cleverly introduces the reader to the world of stereotypes internalized by Filipino women who have learned to externalize their own struggle for independence. Although the "exotic" cannot be removed from these women, they transcend constraining traditions and use them to empower themselves. It is then that they begin to realize the "American Dream" that brought their families to this country.

Women of all ages can relate to these blurred visions of the "American Dream." "Talk to Me, Milagros" examines the harsh political reality of dreams lost because of a family's move to the United States in search of a better life. Galang's writing brings forth the sad beauty and strength of an immigrant family in the twentieth century. The image of Milagros' father *crying, sobbing, sometimes quietly and at other times howl-*

ing, after his pride is shattered when his daughter discovers his *new, American job* is waiting tables at a restaurant, illuminates the suffering and dissolution of dreams faced by an immigrant family in America. The women become the silent foundation of the family in this new American life. A mother's strength, and simultaneous submissiveness to the father's needs and pride, creates an intricate web of traditions being broken and recreated. Milagros' refusal to speak English, while holding steadfastly to Tagalog and her photograph of friends from home, remains her only ties to the culture and traditions of her homeland.

These traditions to which Milagros clings are the same traditions that hinder Galang's other female characters from easily leading successful, independent lives. Galang's world emanates as a mixture of language, sexuality, obedience, virtue, tradition, the role of fathers and tradition-bound mothers, work, pregnancy, and the memories of the Philippines. These ingredients merge into one entity that influences each and every action these women take in their daily lives. Their actions, whether positive or negative (according to their family's values) become a cry for independence from the old, constricting traditions.

Galang's *Her Wild American Self* brings forth many feminist issues that surround women of color. Her stories recall the lives of women of color who are sometimes forgotten and who are not able to move freely in this country called America, land of opportunity. Because of their fear of being ostracized by relatives, friends, and strangers, these Filipino women travel within the shadow of their culture that does not allow them the many choices that are available to Caucasian women in America.

There is no escape for these women from their culture. *From the start, you [are] a piece that [does] not fit, never given the chance to be like the rest—the ones with the blond hair and the red hair and something someone called strawberry.* The characters come alive in these pages when they wake to find that, by redefining traditions to fit new lifestyles, living in America allows them the freedom to choose their own paths. It allows them to continue to hope, to dream, and to relish becoming what their Filipino relatives term a *bratty American.*

Editor's Note: The title story, "Her Wild American Self," was originally published in CALYX Journal, *vol. 16, no. 2.*

TERI MAE RUTLEDGE

SEEING DELL. Carol Guess, Cleis Press, Box 8933, Pittsburgh, PA 15221, 1996, 170 pages, $12.95 paper.

The central character of *Seeing Dell* is absent. Carol Guess' debut novel revolves around Dell, a midwestern taxi driver killed in a car crash. The novel is split into eight sections, from the point of view of five different characters.

The level of connection of each character to Dell differs: two characters, one male and one female, were Dell's lovers. Copeland (appropriately nicknamed "Cope") is unable to stop grieving Dell's death. His grief is vivid, almost tangible. Nightly, he sits on old brown chair, places his feet on an old microwave box, and conjures Dell's face.

Cope is not aware that Dell's friend, Terry Cintos, was also her lover. Terry, a drama teacher at a private high school, climbed into Dell's taxicab one afternoon and forged a relationship that would soon eclipse Dell's feelings for Copeland.

We do this for each other: tug on the skins our friends and lovers need to discard. It's a beautiful thing, but horrible too, because once it's done, you're so often left with the skin and not the body-in-motion. That's what happened to Cope, though she died before he had to face finding out.

Other characters reveal their connection to Dell, Terry, and Cope as their narratives unfold.

Nora, the first lover Cope took after Dell's death, is a deliciously mean barfly. Copeland is entranced by her determination and finds being with her like riding a galloping horse for the first time. He is unable to control where their affair turns, knowing that their break-up could destroy both of them.

She looked quiet; I was afraid of her eyes....
"How I'm feeling?" She stood up and flicked her skirt at me, making it look like an accident, but letting me see the inside of her thigh. Then she bent over the table, put her hands on my shoulders, her face right up in mine. "If I were a man," her lips touched my ear as she spoke, so that I felt her words as much as heard them, "if I were, Copeland, I'd rape you."

Carol Guess revisits the same moment in time from different characters' points of view without sounding tedious. This overlap in time is interesting; she offers a temporal organization that is not chronological, that is even more complicated than flashback narratives. She shows that in one story there are actually many tales, depending on the teller. I appreciate this primacy assigned to characters over events, and I enjoyed what was revealed in the re-telling of situations that illuminated character traits, alliances, and grudges.

The subtle differences in Nora and Copeland's view of the moment of their break-up is a good example of those revelations.

I felt anger fall across my body like a shadow, chilling me even in the overheated room. I wanted to shake him, but most of all I wanted him to want me back. So I used sex then, not because I thought it would work on Copeland, just out of habit. It's the only tool for revenge I know. I flicked my skirt open a little, teasing him. Then I felt my throat tighten, desire and anger rubbing my voice raw. I leaned across the table, took hold of his shoulders. "If you were a man," I said, and I meant it, "Copeland, I'd rape you."

Another of her characters is a former lover of Nora's, James. He is homophobic and bigoted, and his conceptualization of Dell is informed by gossip and speculation. In a satisfying poetically just twist, it is suggested that each of James' two children have homosexual tendencies.

Finally, there is Maureen, who dated Copeland briefly and desperately needs someone to watch over her son for a week. She finally calls Copeland. Her son is a student of Terry Cintos, along with his best friend, James' son.

Seeing Dell demonstrates the complex ways in which people know each other. Carol Guess' characters cannot exist independently. Pieces of them exist in other people's stories, secrets, gossip, and thoughts. The complicated web of relationships surrounding each character in *Seeing Dell* reveals selves much more complex than a singular character's internal ego constructs. The most impressive manifestation of these narrative conversations about other characters is the creation of Dell herself, whose voice is never heard in the novel. Her centrality to the narrative, and her fragmented-yet-complete characterization, result from Guess' finely honed narrative skills.

Hers is a voice that is complex and sophisticated. She is a writer to watch.

MARIA ISABEL RODRIGUEZ

HISPANIC, FEMALE AND YOUNG: AN ANTHOLOGY. Edited by Phyllis Tashlik, Piñata Books, a division of Arte Público Press, University of Houston, Houston, TX 77204-2090, 1994, 217 pages, $14 paper.

A Class like Las Mujeres *is something that helps you learn about yourself and others and find compassion in your heart to appreciate other cultures while finding in yourself who you really are....*

This book is the result of *Las Mujeres*, an innovative class in an east Harlem school that was designed to awaken young Hispanic women to the wealth of their cultures' literary traditions and to their own abilities as writers. The young women read and interviewed a range of Hispanic women they admired, from famous authors to Congresswomen to their own mothers, and wrote at length on their feelings about these experiences. This book is an anthology of some of the essays from the class, as well as selections of the literature that inspired them. The resulting dialogue covers the experiences of being biracial, of coming of age in el barrio, of everyday prejudice, and of success. It includes an array of perspectives from different generations, cultures, and backgrounds that all share the common bond of being Hispanic and female. The diversity of experiences and voices reflected within the selections make this an absorbing book; those selections to which I didn't personally relate were fascinating for the honesty and insight with which they were written. In our multicultural society, second-generation Americans are encouraged to fit into mainstream society, often at the expense of their heritage. *Las Mujeres* is a reminder that those customs that make us different are also a source of pride and support.

Resources

SELECTED BOOKS OF INTEREST

Am I Blue? Marion D. Bauer (HarperCollins, 1995). Short stories for and about bi/lesbian/gay youth.

Black Girl Talk, edited by The Black Girls (Sister Vision Press, 1995). Anthology by black women 15–24 including poetry, prose, essay, dialogue, art work, and photos.

Confessions of the Guerrilla Girls, Guerilla Girls (HarperCollins, 1995). Details how the G.G.—conscience of the art world—got their start. Facts and photos documenting sexism in the art world. (The Girls on the Web: http://www.voyagerco.com/gg)

Daily Chimera, Cole R. Heinowitz (Incommunicado Press, 1995). Collection of poetry, prose, and plays by a 20-year-old woman who "branches into and out of gendered structures...with the deftness of a true visionary."

Departures, Jennifer C. Cornell (University of Pittsburgh Press, 1994). Stories set in Northern Ireland exploring the consequences of struggling to endure violence, loss, failure, and the inability to believe.

Ex Utero, Laurie Foos (Coffee House Press, 1995). "It was at the mall, she believes, that her uterus fell out...." begins Rita's wacky tale of women, men, sexuality, and modern media overkill.

Free Love, Ali Smith (Virago, 1995). Stories about "desire, memory, sexual ambiguity, the imagination...the way things come together and fall apart...in the harsh light of dislocation."

Free Your Mind, Ellen Bass and Kate Kaufman (HarperCollins, 1996). Helpful information for gay/lesbian/bisexual youth.

Girl Power: Young Women Speak Out, edited by Hillary Carlip (Warner Books, 1995). Essays, letters, and writings by teenage women. Includes extensive resource list.

Infanta, Erin Belieu (Copper Canyon, 1995). A first collection of poems that are "portraits, mostly of people caught in ungainly moments of failure and self-revelation."

Jack Kerouac Is Pregnant, Aurelie Sheehan (Dalkey Archive, 1994). Stories of women breaking out— "dreams of misplaced waitresses, prostitutes and other working girls...secretaries too smart to take orders."

Joining the Tribe, edited by Linnea Due (Anchor, 1995). Due traveled across America to ask lesbian, gay, bisexual, and transgender teenagers about their lives. Interviews and social analysis.

Junglee Girl, Ginu Kamani (Aunt Lute, 1995). "Junglee girl" is a South Asian term for a wild and uncontrollable woman—these stories are filled with "bawdiness and explicit sexuality."

Listen Up: Voices from the Next Feminist Generation, edited by Barbara Findlen (Seal Press, 1995). Anthology of "hilarious/funky/fresh/brilliant/angry and crystalline new voices" from a broad spectrum of young feminists.

Mama's Girl, Veronica Chambers (Riverhead Books, 1996). A memoir from Brooklyn in the 1970s; "a meditation on yearning, loss, and the possibilities for growth within a family."

Minus Time, Catherine Bush (Serpent's Tail, 1995). Twenty-year-old Helen's mother's up in space, her father's following natural disasters worldwide, and Helen is left on her own to envision her life.

Monsters and Other Lovers, Lisa Glatt (Pearl Editions, 1995). Glatt writes poems about sex as a female Bukowski, if there were such a person.

Other Women, Evelyn Lau (Simon & Schuster, 1996). The new novel by the twenty-four-year-old author of *Runaway: Diary of a Street Kid , Fresh Girls and Other Stories,* and several poetry collections.

Passion of Alice, The, Stephanie Grant (Houghton-Mifflin, 1995). Debut novel detailing the life of an anorexic woman.

Price of Eggs, The, Anne Panning (Coffee House Press, 1995). Stories of sad children and heartbroken parents written "with a sure hand and a steady eye about the lives of real people in distress."

SurferGrrls: Look Ethel! An Internet Guide for Us! Laurel Gilbert and Crystal Kile (Seal Press, 1996). "Calling all cyberchicks, wired women and girl geek wannabes...." This guide to getting on and using the Internet includes a WWW site of its own.

Sweet Water, Christina Baker Kline (HarperCollins, 1993). A novel about a daughter's search for truth.

Time, The, Esther Iverem (Africa World Press,1993). Poems and photographs that divulge the complexity of an urban African American woman's coming of age in the 1970s &1980s.

When Fox Is a Thousand, Larissa Lai (Press Gang, 1995). "A spellbinding novel about two murders and mysterious coincidences across time."

Wired Women: Gender and New Realities in Cyberspace, edited by Lynn Cherny and Elizabeth Reba Weise (Seal Press, 1996). "Provocative and impassioned look at what women are doing on the net."

SELECTED PUBLICATIONS

Bridges: A Journal for Jewish Feminists and Our Friends, Box 24839, Eugene, OR 97402. Biannual magazine of creative, thoughtful work by Jewish feminists and others.

CHAT, Kings Reach Tower, Stamford St., London, England SE1 9LS. Entertainment magazine for women between 25–34.

Circle, The, 1530 E. Franklin Ave., Minneapolis, MN 55404; (612) 879-1760. Monthly publication of national and local events concerning Native American people. Includes pages written and designed by and for youth.

Factsheet Five, Box 170099, San Francisco, CA , 94117-0099. A guide featuring hundreds of zines, descriptions, where and how to get them.

Foster Care Youth United, 144 W. 27th St., Suite #8R, New York, NY 10001. A monthly newspaper/magazine written by and for young people in foster care.

Fireweed, Box 279 Sta. B, Toronto, ON, Canada M5T 2W2. Feminist journal of writing, politics, art, and culture.

Girltalk, 143 West 96th St., #10D, New York, NY 10025. New comic by women. Launched on flipside of *Real Girl* #7, available from Fantagraphics Books, 7563 Lake City Way NE, Seattle, WA 98115.

Gerll, 656 West Albine #3, Chicago, IL 60657. All-girl fanzine distributor.

HUES (Hear Us Emerging Sisters), Box 7778, Ann Arbor, MI 48107; 1-800-HUES-4U2. Multicultural publication for women 18-30, published by young feminists.

Indigenous Woman, Indigenous Women's Network, Box 174, Lake Elmo, MN 55042. Stories and images from women working for indigenous peoples.

Inside Out, Box 460268, San Francisco, CA 94146. Produced by and for gay and lesbian youth.

Iris: A Journal About Women. The Women's Center, Box 323 HSC, University of Virginia, Charlottesville, VA 22908. Includes fiction, poetry, book reviews, interviews, and feature articles.

National Grange, 1616 H St. NW, Washington, DC 20006. Publications for farmers, farm familes, women, and youth.

New Moon: A Magazine for Girls and Their Dreams, New Moon Publishing, Box 3620, Duluth, MN 55803. A feminist bimonthly edited by 8- to 14-year-old girls.

Outyouth, Y.E.S., The Center, 208 West 13th St., New York, NY 10001. Internationally distributed publication of Youth Enrichment Services, Lesbian and Gay Community Center. A medium for lesbian, bisexual, transgendered, and gay youth.

PLAZM, Box 2863, Portland, OR 97208-2863. Quarterly published by a cooperative of artists dedicated to the unrestricted expression of ideas, beyond the constraints of any one medium.

Prairie Winds, 208 E. Colorado Blvd., Spearfish, SD 57783. Literary and visual arts publications for Native American youth. Sponsors young writers' conferences.

Riot Grrrl Press, 1573 N. Milwaukee Ave. #473, Chicago, IL 60622. All-girl fanzine distributor.

Room of One's Own, Box 46160, Station D, Vancouver, BC, Canada V6J 5G5. Canada's oldest feminist literary journal.

Sinister Wisdom, Box 3252, Berkeley, CA 94703. Multicultural, multi-class journal for the lesbian imagination in the arts and politics.

Teen Voices, Box 6329, Boston, MA 02114. National magazine committed to encouraging teenage and young adult women's expression and empowerment. Written by and for young women.

Thirteenth Moon, Dept. of English, SUNY Albany, Albany, NY 12222. A feminist literary journal.

Two Girls Review, 341 Adams, Eugene, OR 97402. National literary magazine.

Yolk, Informasian Media, Box 861555, Los Angeles, CA 90086. Magazine for the new generation of Asian youth.

Young Voice, Youth Services Group, North York Public Library, Yonge St., North York, ON, Canada M2N 5N9. Magazine for young people's creative work—stories, poems, essays, and drawings.

ORGANIZATIONS

Artsmart, 56 Dolores Terrace, San Francisco, CA, 94110; (415) 255-8691. Offers disadvantaged youth a chance to explore the arts.

Cottages at Hedgebrook: A Retreat for Women Writers, 2197 Millman Rd., Langley, WA 98260. Stays of up to three months. Write for application; deadlines 4/1 & 10/1.

Feminist International Radio Endeavor (FIRE), Box 88, Santa Ana, Costa Rica; (506) 249-18-21; (506) 249-10-95. Broadcasts a two-hour daily program (Spanish and English) on shortwave radio station Radio for Peace International in Costa Rica that is heard in over 100 countries. Invitation to send talks, interviews, stories.

Girls, Inc., 30 East 33rd St., New York, NY 10016; (212) 689-3700. Regional Office-Seattle; (206) 720-2912. Dedicated to serving girls and young women.

International Women's Writing Guild (IWWG), Box 810, Gracie Sta., New York, NY 10028-0082; (212) 737-7536. Women writers in 24 countries interested in expressing themselves.

Lambda Youth Network Leadership, Box 7911, Culver City, CA 90233. List of gay, lesbian, bisexual, and transgender youth help-lines, pen pal programs, & newsletters.

Lambert House Gay Youth Center, 1818 15th Ave, Seattle, WA 98122; (206) 322-2735. Regional drop-in center and support services for lesbian and gay youth.

Lesbian Herstory Educational Foundation (LHEF), Box 1258, New York, NY 10116; (718) 768-3953. Gather, share, and preserve information on the lives and activities of historical and present-day lesbians worldwide.

National Indian Youth Leadership Project, Box 2140, Gallup, NM 87305; (505) 722-9176. To instill cultural values and provide Native youth with opportunities in developing skills for becoming productive citizens, role models.

National Women's History Project (NWHP), 7738 Bell Rd., Windsor, CA 95492; (707) 838-6000. Annual resource catalogue promoting awareness of the history of American women. Sponsors National Women's History month.

Norcroft, Box 300105, Minneapolis, MN 55403. A writing retreat for women for up to four weeks between May & October. Write for application.

Pacific Islander and Asian Resource Gathering, c/o NW Ctr for Equity & Diversity, Edmonds Community College, 20000-68th Ave W, Lynnwood, WA 98036; (206) 640-

1065 or (206) 329-1994. Regional grassroots organization working to provide resources for young women of Pacific Islander and Asian descent. Organizes a Washington statewide conference for high-school age women each year. Serves as an information and resource center, provides referrals, and supports young women.

Third Wave, 185 Franklin St., 3rd floor, New York, NY 10013. Member-driven, national nonprofit devoted to feminist activism for social change; seeks to build a lasting foundation for young women's activism around the country.

Women in the Arts Foundation, 1175 York Ave., Apt. 2G, New York, NY 10021; (212) 751-1915. Women artists and women interested in the arts, working to overcome discrimination and protest under-representation of women artists.

Women for Racial and Economic Equality (WREE), 198 Broadway, Rm. 606, New York, NY 10038; (212) 385-1103. Working to end race discrimination in hiring, pay, and promotion for women of all countries.

Women of Color Resource Center (WCRC), 2288 Fulton Street, Suite 103, Berkeley, CA 94704; (510) 848-9272. Vehicle for dialogue and interchange among women of color about current status and strategies for change. Bridge for activists for racial justice and gender equality. National directory of women-of-color organizations.

Women's Access to Electonic Resources (WATER), 109 Johanna St., Austin, TX 78704; (512) 444-1672; E-mail: water@igc.apc.org. Providing training in video and radio production and in computer networking, WATER exists to provide space for women to acquire electronic communication skills.

YWCA, New York, NY 1003-9595; (212) 614-2700. To empower women, girls, and their families and to eliminate racism.

A SAMPLING OF ONLINE RESOURCES

DC Webgrrls. Practical information on getting on-line and great resource list and links. Provides a forum for women and girls to network. Web: http://www.softaid.net/dcwebgrrls/primer.html

Links for the Discriminating Web Diva. Incredible list of links to women on the Web, including "computer chicks" and "activist resources." Web: http://www.rpi.edu/~schmel/gender.html

NrrdGrrl! Links. Great list of links to women on the Web. Web: http://www.winternet.com/~ameliaw/nrrdlink.html

Queer Resource Center. Web site with links to arts & culture, colleges, organizations, publications, and more. Web: http://www.infoqueer.org/queer/qis/vl-queer.html

Virtual Sisterhood, PO Box 252 , Metuchen, NJ 08840. A global women's electronic support network dedicated to increasing women's access to and effective use of electronic communications. Web: http://www.igc.apc.org/vsister/vsister.html

Contributor Notes

Ruth Adermann (1970)* is writing and working in Orange County (CA) but her heart remains in Arizona. Her work is published or is forthcoming in *Kinesis, Chiron Review, Beehive, Faultline, Misnomer,* and *Coal City Review.* Poetry: "Trinity," p. 156

Cara Judea Alhadeff (1971) earned a BPhil from the University Scholars' Program and the School of Visual Arts, Pennsylvania State University. Her studies combined cultural anthropology, eco-feminism, environmental justice, photography, and performance studies. Art: Untitled, pp. 130 & 131

Margaret Almon (1967), a Moravian who lives near where H.D. was born, was born to two newly middle-class parents and grew up in Canada. She has lived in Massachusetts, Oregon, and Illinois and is a poet and librarian now working in Pennsylvania. Her poetry is published in *two girls review (varieties of violence).* Poetry: "Small Stones," p. 60

Kahlil Sucgang Apuzen (1973) was born in South Cotobato, Philippines. She was inspired by her parents' work in labor unions, grassroots, and women's movements. She immigrated to Florida in 1988 and is studying political science and environmental science at The Evergreen State College (Olympia, WA). Poetry: "learning Philippine history," p. 29, & "Aliens," p. 32

Sarah Avery (1970) grew up on a series of army bases in Japan, Korea, Germany, and the U.S. She studied at Vassar and Johns Hopkins and is now pursuing a PhD in English Literature at Rutgers. She is particularly interested in women poets' rebukes, revisions, and reinventions of sacred narrative. She lives in New Brunswick (NJ). Poetry: "For My Sister at 17," p. 64

Magda Baker (1970) is a Jewish woman raised in South Carolina. She studied printmaking and politics at Bennington College in Vermont. She has lived in Seattle since 1992, and she cleans houses for a living. She has participated in several informal art shows in Seattle. Art: "Gallon of Milk," p. 89

M. M. Bilas (1968) was born in Suba, Fiji. As a child she lived in Australia and New Zealand. She completed her formal education in the U.S. and Canada. She currently lives in a soggy climate and longs for the sun. Prose: "The Floating Sari," p. 50

Deborah L. Blicher (1963) is a graduate student in writing at Emerson College (Boston). She has previously worked as a research psychologist and technical writer. This is her first publication of creative prose. Her most recent publications are two poems in *Fledgling.* Prose: "The Front Lines," p. 68

Laura Cherry (1968) is a freelance technical writer living in Somerville (MA). She earned a BA from Wesleyan University and has attended the Master of Fine Arts program in English at the University of Massachusetts, Amherst. Her work has recently appeared in *Flyway.* Poetry: "On the Bridge," p. 98

Lauri Conner (1969) is a Seattle-based writer who received her MFA from the University of Washington. Her work has appeared in *CATALYST, Point No Point,* and *Revival.* Poetry: "A Father's Child," p. 28

Germaine Curry (1971) was born in Pennsylvania and has lived in sundry places ever since. She earned a BA from the University of Oregon in 1993 and is currently pursuing an MA at the University of Texas, Austin. Poetry: "Stopped at the Tracks," p. 114

* date of birth

Priti Darooka (1965) is an Indian painter living in Seattle. She earned an MFA from the Pratt Institute (Brooklyn, NY). She has lectured and held shows across the country (most recently in Seattle) and in India. **Art: "Nostalgia," p. 34, & "A Landscape for My Mom," p. 35**

An observer of human, aural, and visual life, **Sabrina Davis** (1964) is not ashamed to be called a feminist or lesbian; low-income or uneducated; a sister, drifter, or witch. She paints, writes, plays the guitar, drums, and gardens in order to feel connected and whole. **Art: "From Mother to Son," p. 121**

Mary Beth Deline (1976) is studying film production at Simon Fraser University (BC). She currently gardens a lot and works as an Internet consultant for small businesses. She likes cats, cinnamon hearts, and people who speak their minds. **Poetry: "Melissa Is My Name," p. 84**

Stacey Dressen-McQueen (1970) is a freelance illustrator and embroiderer living in Portland (OR). She was born in South Dakota. **Art: Untitled, pp. 48 & 49**

Lara Karn Frankena (1972) was born in Ann Arbor (MI) and graduated from the University of Michigan, Ann Arbor, in 1994 with a Bachelor's in philosophy, creative writing, and arts and ideas. She is currently living in Brooklyn. **Art: "Theresa," cover**

Alma García (1970) is a half-bred Mexican Swede living in Albuquerque. Although she has been employed as a magazine and newspaper editor in the past, she is currently working three slackeresque jobs and will soon begin pursuing her MFA in creative writing. **Poetry: "Comiendoselo a los muertos (Eating Your Dead)," p. 26**

Dorothy Eileen Goode (1969) earned a BFA from Northern Arizona University (Flagstaff). She has kept alive since then and spent much time looking long into dark places for what images she has found through paint and pencil. She is certain that it is now time for them to be brought to light. **Art: "Untitled, October 1993," p. 142**

Ann E. Green (1968) grew up on a dairy farm in rural Pennsylvania. She currently studies American and working-class women writers at SUNY Albany and hopes to have both her PhD and her first book in print by sometime around her thirtieth birthday. **Prose: "Selling Out: Reflections of a Farm Daughter," p. 90**

Nancy Havlick (1970) earned a BA in studio art from Wake Forest University (Winston-Salem, NC) and lives in Portland (OR). **Art: "Rhythm Unbroken," p. 88**

Kristin Herbert (1968) earned an MFA in poetry from the University of Pittsburgh, where she taught creative writing. Her poetry won an Academy of American Poets Prize and has appeared in numerous journals. She lives in Louisville (KY) and is marketing director at Sarabande Books. **Poetry: "Conceiving of Me," p. 24**

Rebecca Holden (1967) was born in St. Paul (MN). She has worked as a freelance photographer, writing tutor, and photography instructor. She is a graduate student at the University of Wisconsin, Madison, writing her dissertation on feminism and feminist science fiction. **Art: "Krakow, 1994," p. 66 & "Anniversary," p. 67**

Kristin King (1970) earned an MFA from the University of Washington. She was finalist in the 1993 Writers at Work short story competition and received honorable mention in the 1993 Utah Arts Council short story competition. Her work is published in *Parting Gifts*. She lives in Salt Lake City. **Prose: "The Wings," p. 145**

Jennifer Kircher (1970) grew up in upstate New York, then moved to Boston to pursue her MFA at Emerson College. She is a recipient of the Sophie de Liedel Fellowship for short fiction, sponsored by *Ploughshares*, and works as a technical writer in Boston, where she lives with her fiancé, Shaun, and her cat, Maggie. **Prose: "Eastern Frontier," p. 36**

Nomy Lamm (1975) is a "white/Jewish middle class queer/fat/disabled 20-year-old girl" who is a student at The Evergreen State College (WA). She has been published in *Hues* and *Ms.* and in her own zines, and her work is included in *Listen Up: Voices from the Next Generation* (Seal Press, 1995) and *Girl Power: Young Women Speak Out!* (Warner, 1995). Prose: "not my teenage dream," p. 132

Rebecca Lavine (1968) lives in Boston with her dog Gilda. She is a big believer in merging a post-identity queer ideology with the principles of "traditional feminism." She is interested in building a multicultural progressive community of deviants, activists, and artists. Prose: "Afterward," p. 123

Emily Lloyd (1974) was born in Washington (DC). A freelancer and student, her current obsessions include poetry theatre, creative activism, and gender theory. Her work is forthcoming in *Contempory Lesbian Love Poems* (Ballantine Books, 1997). Poetry: "My Breasts: Two Views," p. 140

A performance artist and writer, **Zelda Lockhart** (1965) has published poetry and fiction in various newspapers, magazines, and journals, including *Sinister Wisdom* and *Word Writes*. She is busy promoting her first book of poems, *Fifth Born of Eight*. She is in the middle of moving to Ithaca (NY) where she will finish work on her first novel. Prose: "Mulberry Tree," p. 116

Cathy Malia Lowenberg (1972) is the only daughter of Mary Kobayashi of Honolulu (HI) and Tim Lowenberg of Donnellson (IA). She graduated from the University of Washington in 1995 and works in Seattle as a labor union organizer. Prose: "Excisions of the Flesh," p. 14

Susan Marshall (1965) received an MFA in film and video production from The University of Iowa. She designed and taught workshops for the local Arts Share Program and, most recently, accepted a James A. Michener Fellowship for poetry and screenwriting at The Texas Center for Writers, The University of Texas, Austin. Poetry: "one minute filled," p. 122

Laurie McKiernan (1968) is a performance artist, writer, and painter who settled in Minneapolis eight years ago after eighteen moves before the age of twenty. This is only the second time her work has appeared in a publication she did not photocopy, staple, and hand out herself. Poetry: "400 south 5th street," p. 79, & "onions," p. 83

R. Teri Memolo (1972) is a graduate of the Corcoran School of Art. She is is a writer and photographer for *Herb Magazine*. Her next project is creating seven-foot portraits using 3" x 5" snapshots. Art: Untitled, pp. 105 & 106

Carrie Mesrobian (1975) is a graduate of St. Olaf College in Northfield (MN). She lives and teaches in Minneapolis. Poetry: "The Sun Goes Down in the Suburbs," p. 99

Andrea Nicolich (1970) was born and raised in northern New Jersey. She received a BFA from the School of Visual Arts in New York City. She has had two solo exhibitions and has participated in numerous group shows on the east coast. Art: "I Wear Your Ring," p. 144

Monica Nuvamsa (1976) is an enrolled member of the Hopi tribe who lives in Tucson. She studies psychology at the University of Arizona and plans to attend graduate school for clinical psychology. The themes that permeate her work are based upon her experiences in traditional and contemporary Hopi society. Art: Untitled, p. 155

Debbra Palmer (1968) is a recent graduate of Portland State University (OR). She works for The Oregon Museum of Science and Industry and lives with her partner and two striped cats in Northeast Portland. Her favorite poet is Naomi Shihab Nye. Poetry: "Wade's Hoggers," p. 136, & "Victoria Told Me Her Secret," p. 138

"Born the color of a burnt corndog on Groundhog Day, it would only be a matter of time before **Julianna Parr** (1972) would emerge as outlaw writer and drawer of undiscovered specialty. Sometimes she feels vacuous. Nutshell rendition: some-such ethnic lesbian, toying with ink nibs in roosterland, USA." **Prose: "Avocado Security," p. 107, & Art: "Dream of a Queerbit Fiend," p. 111**

Born and raised on a Wyoming ranch, **Nonie Proffit** (1967) earned a BS in English from Utah State University. An out lesbian with strong ties to the land, she is a librarian in her Wyoming hometown where she lives with her partner of six years. **Poetry: "Nightshift," p. 86**

A native Oregonian, **Dora Alicia Ramirez** (1973) earned a BA in Literature from Oregon State University. She is currently pursuing an MA in English Literature at New Mexico State University. **Review: *Her Wild American Self* by M. Evelina Galang, p. 158**

Nicole M. Rawlins (1971) lives in Portland (OR). She earned her BFA in painting and printmaking from Oregon State University. She is a member of the Northwest Print Council, has won their 1993 printmaking grant, and has been appointed to their board of directors. She works at Inkling Studio, a printmaking cooperative. **Art: "Salome," p. 58**

Leslie Riibe (1969) grew up in Seattle and moved to Chicago last year after graduating from The Evergreen State College. **Art: "Nightgown," p. 143**

Becky Rodia's (1971) first book review appeared last summer in *Quarterly West*. Her poetry has been published in *The Cream City Review, The Laurel Review, Willow Springs,* and elsewhere. Adastra Press will publish her chapbook *Another Fire* in 1997. **Review: *Girl Soldier* by Denise Duhamel, p. 157**

Maria Isabel Rodriguez (1977) is a Corvallis (OR) resident whose interests include reading, snowboarding, and writing. She will be starting her junior year this fall as a general science major at the University of Oregon. **Review: *Hispanic, Female and Young: An Anthology* edited by Phyllis Tashlik, p. 162**

Juliette Torrez (1967) is a spoken word/slam performer and coordinator living in Albuquerque (NM). Her work is published in *Flipside, Manila, Hembra, Kink,* and *Spin Online*. She edited the anthology *Revival: Spoken Word from Lollapalooza '94* (Manic D Press). **Poetry: "TV Child," p. 112**

Jana Unkel (1979) is a senior at Lexington High School (MA). She has been writing poetry for about three years. **Poetry: "growth," p. 62**

Emily Regan Wills (1981) is an eighth grader at Springton Lake Middle School in Media (PA). She has been writing since first grade, when she edited a school magazine. Besides writing, she also pursues drama, singing, and the sciences. **Prose: "The Trip from HECK: Day Two, Wednesday, 8/16," p. 100**

Katherine Wise (1972) earned a BA in creative writing from Miami University (OH). She is studying law at the Ohio State University College of Law (Columbus). She has had poetry published in *Polaris, The Beloit Poetry Journal, Nexus,* and *Inklings*. **Poetry: "excerpt from the law school mailbox sex poems," p. 141**

Alex Zaphiris (1971) identifies herself as a "left-handed, vegetarian, queer-feminist, youngest daughter of Greek-Cypriot immigrant parents." She is interested in the relationships between photography and healing and plans to study osteopathy. She savors ripe hachiya persimmons and currently works in film production. **Art: "Kelly," p. 59**

Editor Notes

Amy Agnello (1970) is a contributing editor for CALYX. She was a member of the editorial collective and the promotions coordinator for CALYX Books from 1992 to 1994. She earned a BA in creative writing, multicultural literature, and history from The Evergreen State College (Olympia, WA). She is currently an advocate and administrator for women and children who are victims of domestic and sexual violence at an agency in Olympia.

Maria Francesca Braganza (1966) is a media artist and educator living and working in Seattle. Her specific interests in media work are experimental documentary, autobiographical film and video, and media installation art. She teaches video to at-risk youth and believes video has a transformative power for young people to tell their own stories. She is a graduate of The Evergreen State College and also attended Oberlin College and the School of Visual Arts for her undergraduate work. Maria is third generation Filipina-American.

Sonia Gomez (1970) is a Sri Lankan who was born in the U.S., but grew up in Kenya and Zimbabwe in a Catholic-Buddhist family. She lives in Seattle and has recently completed an MFA in creative writing at the University of Washington. Her work has been published in *Many Mountains Moving, Zimbabwe Women Writers' Anthology, Emeralds in the Ash,* and *Timberline.* Her poetry has won the Charles Johnson Literary Award and the Walter Kidd Literary Award.

Laura McFarland (1967) is a contributing editor for CALYX and has been a volunteer there for seven years. She has also served as acting editorial coordinator. She has a BA in history and English from the University of California, Santa Barbara and earned an MA in history at the age of twenty-two from the University of Texas, Austin; her thesis topic was the history of midwifery in Early Modern Europe. She was raised by transplanted Texan academicians/farmers in Oregon and now resides in Seattle. Her work has been published in *Midwifery Today.*

Zola M. Mumford (1968), an African-American Louisiana native, lived and traveled in different Asian countries with her family before settling in Seattle. Her film *Charm School* has been featured in several U.S. and Canadian festivals and on television broadcasts. Mumford completed the film *Dear Little Sweet Thang 'Nita* in 1995 for the Seattle Arts Commission's Seattle Artists' Program. She also works on independent productions by other filmmakers, including documentary work for national broadcast for public television, is currently developing a short film for children, and is an avid dancer, reader, and Internet explorer.

Micki Reaman (1963) is the managing editor for this project and the editorial co-coordinator at CALYX. She has been a member of the journal and book editorial collectives since 1992. She earned a BA in contemporary literature and feminist theory from The Evergreen State College. She has worked as a bookseller, a mushroom picker, a fisheries technician, and a freelance desktop publisher.

Teri Mae Rutledge (1972) has been CALYX's promotions coordinator for a year. She has been an intern, volunteer, and journal editor at CALYX since 1993. She earned a BPhil from Miami University's School of Interdisciplinary Studies, with a minor in women's studies and a focus in creative writing. She worked, in different capacities, on four undergraduate publications. Since moving to the Northwest, she has nurtured an obsession with Gore-Tex and espresso, but not snowboarding. **Review: *Seeing Dell*** by Carol Guess, p. 160

Mira Chieko Shimabukuro (1972) is an Okinawan American poet born and raised in Portland (OR), where she began writing in high school. Her poems have been published in *The Raven Chronicles, Coffeehouse Poets' Quarterly, The International Examiner, and Writing For Our Lives.* She currently lives in Seattle where she is an MFA candidate in creative writing at the University of Washington.

Megan Smith (1968) graduated with a degree in art and a minor in Russian studies from Colorado College. Since moving to Portland (OR), she has worked in a variety of preschool-age programs, where she works to help build children's sense of worth, self expression, and exploratory spirit through art and creative projects. Her most recent artwork includes pottery and designing blank cards.

photo by Maria Francesca Braganza

The CALYX Young Women's Editorial Collective
bottom row, l to r: Teri Mae, Maria, Megan; *middle:* Laura, Mira, Zola; *top:* Micki, Sonia, Amy

Selected Titles from Award-Winning CALYX Books

NONFICTION

Natalie on the Street by Ann Nietzke. A day-by-day account of the author's relationship with an elderly homeless woman who lived on the streets of Nietzke's central Los Angeles neighborhood. *PEN West Finalist.*
ISBN 0-934971-41-2, $14.95, paper; ISBN 0-934971-42-0, $24.95, cloth.

The Violet Shyness of Their Eyes: Notes from Nepal by Barbara J. Scot. A moving account of a western woman's transformative sojourn in Nepal as she reaches mid-life. *PNBA Book Award.*
ISBN 0-934971-35-8, $14.95, paper; ISBN 0-934971-36-6, $24.95, cloth.

In China with Harpo and Karl by Sibyl James. Essays revealing a feminist poet's experiences while teaching in Shanghai, China.
ISBN 0-934971-15-3, $9.95, paper; ISBN 0-934971-16-1, $17.95, cloth.

FICTION

Into the Forest, by Jean Hegland. This novel is a glimpse into the near-future. In gripping prose, Hegland details the collapse of society and the struggle of two teenage sisters to survive alone in the Northern California forest.
ISBN 0-934971-49-8, $13.95, paper; ISBN 0-934971-50-1, $25.95, cloth.

Four Figures in Time by Patricia Grossman. This novel tracks the lives of four characters in a New York City art school. It's full of astute observations on modern life as the rarefied world of making art meets the mundane world of making ends meet.
ISBN 0-934971-47-1, $13.95, paper; ISBN 0-934971-48-X, $25.95, cloth.

The Adventures of Mona Pinsky by Harriet Ziskin. In this fantastical novel, a 65-year-old Jewish woman, facing alienation and ridicule, comes of age and ultimately is reborn on a heroine's journey.
ISBN 0-934971-43-9, $12.95, paper; ISBN 0-934971-44-7, $24.95, cloth.

Killing Color by Charlotte Watson Sherman. These compelling, mythical short stories by a gifted storyteller explore the African-American experience. *Washington Governor's Award.*
ISBN 0-934971-17-X, $9.95, paper; ISBN 0-934971-18-8, $19.95, cloth.

Mrs. Vargas and the Dead Naturalist by Kathleen Alcalá. Fourteen stories set in Mexico and the Southwestern U.S., written in the tradition of magical realism.
ISBN 0-934971-25-0, $9.95, paper; ISBN 0-934971-26-9, $19.95, cloth.

Ginseng and Other Tales from Manila by Marianne Villanueva. Poignant short stories set in the Philippines. *Manila Critic's Circle National Literary Award Nominee.*
ISBN 0-934971-19-6, $9.95, paper; ISBN 0-934971-20-X, $19.95, cloth.

POETRY

Another Spring, Darkness: Selected Poems of Anuradha Mahapatra translated by Carolyne Wright et.al. The first English translation of poetry by this working-class woman from West

Bengal. "These are burning poems, giving off a spell of light...."—Linda Hogan
ISBN 0-934971-51-X, $12.95 paper; ISBN 0-934971-52-8, $23.95, cloth.

The Country of Women by Sandra Kohler. A collection of poetry that explores woman's experience as sexual being, as mother, as artist. Kohler finds art in the mundane, the sacred, and the profane.
ISBN 0-934971-45-5, $11.95, paper; ISBN 0-934971-46-3, $21.95, cloth.

Light in the Crevice Never Seen by Haunani-Kay Trask. This first book of poetry by an indigenous Hawaiian to be published in North America is about a Native woman's love for her land, and the inconsolable grief and rage that come from its destruction.
ISBN 0-934971-37-4, $11.95, paper; ISBN 0-934971-38-2, $21.95, cloth.

Open Heart by Judith Mickel Sornberger. An elegant collection of poetry rooted in a woman's relationships with family, ancestors, and the world.
ISBN 0-934971-31-5, $9.95, paper; ISBN 0-934971-32-3, $19.95, cloth.

Raising the Tents by Frances Payne Adler. A personal and political volume of poetry, documenting a Jewish woman's discovery of her voice.
ISBN 0-934971-33-1, $9.95, paper; ISBN 0-934971-34-X, $19.95, cloth.

Black Candle: Poems about Women from India, Pakistan, and Bangladesh by Chitra Divakaruni. Lyrical and honest poems that chronicle significant moments in the lives of South Asian women. *Gerbode Award.*
ISBN 0-934971-23-4, $9.95, paper; ISBN 0-934971-24-2, $19.95 cloth.

Indian Singing in 20th Century America by Gail Tremblay. A brilliant work of hope by a Native American poet.
ISBN 0-934971-13-7, $9.95, paper; ISBN 0-934971-14-5, $19.95, cloth.

Idleness Is the Root of All Love by Christa Reinig, translated by Ilze Mueller. These poems by the prize-winning German poet accompany two older lesbians through a year together in love and struggle.
ISBN 0-934971-21-8, $10, paper; ISBN 0-934971-22-6, $18.95, cloth.

ANTHOLOGIES

The Forbidden Stitch: An Asian American Women's Anthology edited by Shirley Geok-lin Lim, et al. The first Asian American women's anthology. *American Book Award.*
ISBN 0-934971-04-8, $16.95, paper; ISBN 0-934971-10-2, $32, cloth.

Women and Aging, An Anthology by Women edited by Jo Alexander, et al. The only anthology that addresses ageism from a feminist perspective. A rich collection of older women's voices.
ISBN 0-934971-00-5, $15.95, paper; ISBN 0-934971-07-2, $28.95, cloth.

*CALYX Books are available to the trade from Consortium
and other major distributors and jobbers.*

*Individuals may order direct from CALYX Books, P.O. Box B, Corvallis, OR 97339. Send
check or money order in U.S. currency; add $1.50 postage for first book, $.75 each
additional book. Credit card orders only: FAX to 541-753-0515
or call toll-free 1-888-FEM BOOK*

CALYX, A Journal of Art and Literature by Women

CALYX, A Journal of Art and Literature by Women, has showcased the work of over two thousand women artists and writers since 1976. Committed to providing a forum for *all* women's voices, *CALYX* presents diverse styles, images, issues, and themes which women writers and artists are exploring.

CALYX holds a special place in my heart. Some of my very first published words—two poems—were published in CALYX years ago. I've never forgotten the thrill of turning those beautifully illustrated pages and seeing my name, my earnest words, printed there alongside those of some of my literary heroines. It made me feel as if I belonged to the important company of women.
— Barbara Kingsolver

The work you do brings dignity, intelligence, and a sense of wholeness to the world. I am only one of many who bows respectfully—
to all of you and to your work.
—Barry Lopez

Published in June and November; three issues per volume.

CALYX Journal is available to the trade from Ingram Periodicals and other major distributors.

CALYX Journal is available at your local bookstore or direct from:

CALYX, Inc., P.O. Box B, Corvallis, OR 97339

 CALYX Books and CALYX Journal

CALYX is committed to producing books of literary, social, and feminist integrity.

CALYX, Inc., is a nonprofit organization with a 501(C)(3) status.
All donations are tax deductible.

Colophon
The text of this book was composed in Optima with titles in Futura Condensed.

Page layout and composition provided by ImPrint Services, Corvallis, Oregon.